"I Thought You Would Be Ruthless And Arrogant And Full Of Yourself."

"What makes you think I'm not?"

For a second she stared back at him, knocked off balance by the impact of that question. Low, quiet, dangerous. "Last night," she told him, recovering. Lifting her chin. "You know you could have had me."

Heat flashed in his eyes. "I know."

And while she was still dealing with all the conflicting implications of that statement, he leaned down and kissed her.

Oh, man. He kissed her.

The response was instant. Her complete sensory system quivered. She drew in his scent. Not yesterday's cologne but the musky impression of man.

Not the filthy-rich tycoon, not the ruthless groom, just the man.

Dear Reader,

It's November and perhaps the weather is turning a bit cooler where you are...so why not heat things up with six wonderful Silhouette Desire novels? *New York Times* bestselling author Diana Palmer is back this month with a LONG, TALL TEXANS story not to be missed. You've loved Blake Kemp and his ever-faithful assistant, Violet, in other books.... Now you finally get their love story, in *Boss Man*.

Heat continues to generate in DYNASTIES: THE ASHTONS with Laura Wright's contribution, *Savor the Seduction*. Grant and Anna shared a night of passion some months ago...now he's wondering if they have a shot at a repeat performance. And the temperature continues to rise as Sara Orwig delivers her share of surprises, in *Highly Compromised Position*, the latest installment in the TEXAS CATTLEMAN'S CLUB: THE SECRET DIARY series. (Hint, someone in Royal, Texas, is pregnant!)

Brenda Jackson gets things simmering in *The Chase Is On*, another fabulous Westmoreland story with a strong emphasis on food...tasty! And Bronwyn Jameson is back with the conclusion of her PRINCES OF THE OUTBACK series. Who wouldn't want to share body heat with *The Ruthless Groom?* Last but not least, get all hot and bothered in the boardroom with Margaret Allison's business-becomes-pleasure holiday story, *Mistletoe Maneuvers*.

Here's hoping you find plenty of ways to keep yourself warm. Enjoy all we have to offer at Silhouette Desire.

Best,

Melissa Jeglinski

Melissa Jeglinski
Senior Editor
Silhouette Books

Please address questions and book requests to:
Silhouette Reader Service
U.S.: 3010 Walden Ave., P.O. Box 1325, Buffalo, NY 14269
Canadian: P.O. Box 609, Fort Erie, Ont. L2A 5X3

THE
RUTHLESS
GROOM

BRONWYN
JAMESON

Silhouette®

Desire

Published by Silhouette Books

America's Publisher of Contemporary Romance

This, my tenth book, I dedicate to the wonderful editors who made it happen, Leslie Wainger and Stacy Boyd. Ladies, your blood is worth bottling!

 SILHOUETTE BOOKS

ISBN 0-373-76691-2

THE RUTHLESS GROOM

Copyright © 2005 by Bronwyn Turner

Visit Silhouette Books at www.eHarlequin.com

Printed in U.S.A.

Books by Bronwyn Jameson

Silhouette Desire

In Bed with the Boss's Daughter #1380
Addicted to Nick #1410
Zane: The Wild One #1452
Quade: The Irresistible One #1487
A Tempting Engagement #1571
Beyond Control #1596
Just a Taste #1645
*The Rugged Loner #1666
*The Rich Stranger #1680
*The Ruthless Groom #1691

*Princes of the Outback

BRONWYN JAMESON

spent much of her childhood with her head buried in a book. As a teenager, she discovered romance novels, and it was only a matter of time before she turned her love of reading them into a love of writing them. Bronwyn shares an idyllic piece of the Australian farming heartland with her husband and three sons, a thousand sheep, a dozen horses, assorted wildlife and one kelpie dog. She still chooses to spend her limited downtime with a good book. Bronwyn loves to hear from readers. Write to her at bronwyn@bronwynjameson.com.

OUTBACK GLOSSARY

bitumen—tar, as used to seal roads

Brunswick—inner suburb of Melbourne

the bush—the country (as opposed to the city)

cabbie—taxi driver

Dandenongs—mountain range near Melbourne

Flemington—racetrack, home of the Melbourne Cup

Kameruka Downs—outback cattle station, or ranch; the Carlisle home

Kookaburras—Australian laughing birds

Melbourne—Australia's second largest city

Melbourne Cup—(a.k.a. "The Cup" and "the big one" and "the race that stops a nation") Australia's richest horse race, held the first Tuesday of November

muster—round-up

Port Phillip Bay—Melbourne is built around this huge bay

razoo—Aussie slang, a coin of little value

ropeable—very angry

Tim Tams—chocolate-coated cookies (the perfect PMS remedy!)

trams—streetcars; public transport in Melbourne

truckies—truckers/truck drivers

One

I'm sorry, Alex, but I can't marry you today.

Usually it took a lot more than a single line of print to shake Alex Carlisle's carefully constructed composure, but that particular line leaped off the innocent sheet of paper and rocked him like a thunderbolt.

Jilted. Two hours before he was due to sign the marriage contract. And he hadn't glimpsed a hint of it coming.

The rest of Susannah's *I-need-some-space-and-time-to-think, I'm-sorry* explanation swam before his eyes in a swamping tide of frustration. To hell with apologies. He didn't need an explanation; he needed a wife in his bed.

Tonight, if not sooner.

"Is everything all right, sir?"

Easing his crumpling grip on the page, Alex nodded to the hotel concierge who'd handed him the message. "Thank you, Emilio. Yes."

Everything would be all right, Alex decided, setting his jaw as the first wave of reaction subsided. Once he found Susannah and got to the bottom of what the hell had changed since yesterday when they'd last spoken.

Last-minute jitters, that's all it could be. Even serene, sensible Susannah had a right to wedding-day nerves, right? Especially with the importance of what the marriage entailed to Alex and his family weighty on her shoulders.

Carefully his fingers smoothed over the note, then folded it along the existing crease lines. She'd known about his father's will from the start. He'd been honest and direct about his immediate need for a baby to satisfy that clause…or to satisfy his determination to fulfill that clause.

One baby between the three Carlisle half brothers, conceived within three months. That's "all" Charles Carlisle had asked for, and they'd made a pact, he and his brothers. One-in, all-in, to increase the odds of success.

As the eldest he considered it his duty, his responsibility, made all the more pressing by his brothers' lack of success to date. Not that that surprised him. Neither Tomas nor Rafe had tackled the problem with a strategy. Neither Tomas nor Rafe had wanted the marriage/family/baby deal.

Alex did.

He wanted his baby born within a family unit. He wanted a wife and he'd chosen Susannah, a friend and business associate, for all the right reasons. She just needed reminding of those reasons.

Discreetly the concierge cleared his throat. "The flowers were delivered to your suite half an hour ago, Mr. Carlisle. And the delivery from Cartier has been put in the hotel safe for security. I believe everything is now in order."

Everything was in order for the low-key exchange of vows they'd chosen because of the short time frame and because neither of them had wanted a media scrum. Everything was in order except for the bride.

"There is one more thing." Alex snapped his brain out of contemplation and into action. "My fiancée may be late. See if the officiant can block out a longer period of time this afternoon."

"How much longer, sir?"

"Indefinite. But I'll make any inconvenience worth her while."

"Yes, sir."

"I'll need my car out front in ten minutes." To go and fetch Susannah from wherever she'd taken those last-minute jitters. Hopefully her mother would know. Or one of her employees. "I have some phone calls to make and then I'm going out. But if the lady who delivered this note ..."

"Zara."

"Susannah," he corrected, frowning.

"I believe she's a friend of your fiancée, sir. Zara Lovett. She dropped off the envelope on her way to work."

Alex's inner tension loosened a notch, then strengthened with a new sense of purpose. If this friend delivered the note, she must know Susannah's whereabouts. "Do you know where Zara Lovett works?"

"Of course, sir. She's a personal trainer with an agency we secure quite often for our guests. I have her card on file."

Susannah wasn't here.

Botheration.

Zara Lovett's leather-clad shoulders slumped a tad as she completed a second slow circuit of the cabin on her motorbike. No vehicle lurked around the back; no windows lay open to air. The single-room hut sat crouched in the center of its cleared mountain block, still sleeping off a prolonged winter hibernation. The only sign of life was the choral chortle of kookaburras in one of the mountain gums.

Laughing, no doubt, at her wasted efforts.

A two-and-a-half-hour ride out from Melbourne, ten bucks blown on a lousy roadhouse lunch, and all for nothing. She'd been so certain Susannah would be here. When her one o'clock client hadn't shown at the inner-city gym as arranged, she'd considered it a sign and a blessing.

With a whole afternoon on her hands, she could do something about the worry fretting away at the back of her brain.

Her worry wasn't over Susannah calling off today's wedding. For that she'd raised a heartfelt hallelujah. No, her concern centered on the out-of-character suddenness of Susannah's decision and the fact that she'd gone incommunicado. Susannah, who didn't go to the bathroom without at least one phone!

That's why Zara had thought of the cabin. It belonged to Susannah's grandfather and was the only place Zara could imagine her going that didn't boast communication facilities. And her early morning message—a harried-sounding voice-mail asking Zara to deliver a letter to her fiancé's hotel—had mentioned going away somewhere to think.

Zara had spent time up here herself for just that purpose. When it came to escaping, to thinking about one's life direction, this cabin was a tried and tested location.

She slowed her bike to a stop, turned off the engine and kicked down the stand. She might as well stretch her legs and fill her lungs with some clean high-country air before heading back to the city. After shucking gloves and helmet, she unzipped her jacket…then zipped it back up again when the wind snapped at her bare skin.

So much for the gorgeous spring day she'd left behind in Melbourne. Squinting up at the cloud-laced sky, she decided to limit her walk to a brisk five minutes. Then she'd be out of here if this fickle weather decided to blow up a storm.

A flash of…something…through the trees caught her attention as she prepared to dismount. Staring into the thick bushland, she waited until the gleam reappeared and took form as the highly polished panels of a car. A second later she heard the motor, heard it slow to turn in to the cabin, and she released her breath on a slow puff of relief.

"About time, Suse."

Her gaze narrowed on the dark vehicle as it crawled into view. The same prestigious European badge, the same darkly tinted glass, the same sleek lines, but a bigger, gutsier model than Susannah's.

And that definitely wasn't Susannah behind the wheel, she decided, as the car purred to a halt ten yards away. The driver's door opened and a man stepped out. Zara's heart did a half kick against her ribs.

Alex Carlisle.

Although they'd never met, she recognized him instantly. She noted that his dark suit looked as sleek and expensively European as the vehicle. Noted his broad shoulders and flat stomach as he buttoned his jacket over a crisp white shirt.

Noted how his gaze fixed on her without hesitation.

Zara had seen his picture often enough to know those eyes were the same blue-gray as a winter storm on Port Phillip Bay. She imagined they were just as cold and forbidding. Despite her leathers, goose bumps shivered over her skin as his car door snapped shut with a decisive note.

Yep, that was definitely Alex Carlisle cutting down the distance between them with long, purpose-filled strides. But what on earth was he doing out here? How did he even know about this place?

Boots planted solidly on either side of her bike, she lifted her chin and prepared to ask. Then their eyes met with a force that licked through her body like electric flame and fried her questions on the spot. By the time her synapses recovered, she'd lost the advantage. By then his gaze had narrowed a fraction, deepening the creases at the corners of his eyes. "You're Zara Lovett?"

"That's right."

He nodded, a brief, terse acknowledgment, before asking, "Where's Susannah?"

He certainly didn't waste any time getting to the point. Or any breath introducing himself. Zara supposed when your picture appeared pretty much daily somewhere in Australia's press, you assumed recognition. "I don't know," she said in answer to his question.

His gaze shifted, sliding over the cabin and its surroundings in one measuring sweep before returning to her. "She's not here?"

Zara shook her head, which he might or might not have caught since he'd started walking, past her and up onto the cabin's porch. "Don't you believe me?" she called after him, turning to watch as he peered in one window, then the second.

Hands on hips, he turned. "Your boyfriend told me you'd come out here to find her."

Her *what?* Zara opened her mouth and closed it again. He could only mean her housemate, Tim. Which meant— "You rang my home? How did you get my number?"

"Does that matter?"

"Yes. Yes, it does."

"No," he countered with the same certainty. "What matters is locating Susannah. Where is she, Zara?"

"I don't understand. Didn't you get the note I left at your hotel?"

"I don't understand why *you* left the note."

"Because Susannah asked me to."

"Don't play games with me, Zara." Something glinted in his eyes, a fierceness at odds with his even tone. "I am not in the mood to play nice."

"Are you ever?"

"When I want to—" he said, deceptively soft, deceptively smooth, as he started toward her "—I can be very nice."

"I guess I'll have to take your word for that."

When he stepped off the porch, Zara's pulse skipped. Not nerves, but the same kind of adrenaline spike that used to accompany her onto the mat before a fight. Especially one with an expert opponent.

Time, she decided, to get off her bike.

At six foot in her biker boots, Zara was used to setting men back on their heels just by standing and meeting their eyes. Alex Carlisle stood an inch or two taller and he met her gaze without a flicker of surprise. Zara looked right back and for a moment got lost in the intensity of his eyes. Not exactly blue, too vivid to be gray, and with a dark rim around the iris that sucked you into their powerful focus.

And it struck her, in that long, silent sizing-up moment, that it would take a lot to put Alex Carlisle on the ropes. That once he set his mind to something he would follow through with ruthless purpose. She didn't mind that in a person—in fact she liked purpose, she liked directness, she liked a spark of go-get-'em—but, oh, Susannah.

Now I understand your reluctance to tell him face-to-face. You wouldn't have stood a chance.

"Let's start over," he said in that same low voice. "I'm sorry I came on so strong. It's been a hell of a day."

Then he smiled and offered his hand and his name, and she realized why Susannah might have been persuaded into such a coldhearted marriage arrangement. *He's not so cold,* she realized, as the heat from his grip and the impact of that smile seeped into her blood.

"When you saw Susannah this morning—"

"No." She extracted her hand and smoothed it down her thigh. She really, really hoped the sparks she felt were only static electricity. "I didn't see her. I didn't even speak to her. She left a message on my machine, then she e-mailed the letter I left at your hotel."

Irritation pinched between his dark brows. "Why couldn't she call me? Tell me herself?"

"She said she tried to contact you this morning, before you left Sydney."

"Yet here I am."

A six-hundred-mile plane trip from his home in another state. Yet Zara didn't think the inconvenience of a wasted journey played any part in the darkened intensity of his eyes, the flare of his nostrils. For the first time, she let herself see his side of this picture. Effectively left at the altar, he had a right to some anger, some hurt and some answers.

"Suse really did try," she said on a softer note. "Her message to me sounded all flustered because she hadn't been able to contact you. When she said she was going somewhere to think, when I couldn't get her on her mobile phone, I thought she'd come up here."

"Flustered doesn't sound like Susannah."

"No, but then everything about this situation is unlike Susannah."

"Meaning?"

Zara shrugged. "Suse is careful, a bit cautious, then out

of the blue she decided to marry you. No offense, but I thought your relationship was all about business."

"We'd dated."

"Once or twice? That's hardly grounds for marriage!"

"Don't you think that's between Susannah and me?" His voice turned icy, as chill as the wind that buffeted her jacket hard against her back and whipped her hair across her face.

Impatiently she captured the long strands in one hand. "Yes, it is, but I can't ignore the way she sounded on the phone and the fact she changed her mind overnight."

His eyes narrowed. "You saw her last night?"

"We had dinner. And she sounded dead set on marrying you then."

There must have been something in her tone or her expression, because his narrow gaze sharpened on her face. "Dead set in spite of your views on what constitutes grounds for marriage?"

"I didn't force Susannah to do anything, if that's what you're implying."

"You only…what…suggested she take some more time to think about it?"

"That was my advice." Zara met his eyes without apology. They darkened with a ruthless determination that sent a frisson of alarm skittering through her bones. "Why did you come up here? Why were you looking for me?"

"To find Susannah. I have an officiant on standby."

Oh, no, he was not going to bully Susannah into this. Not if she could help it!

When he turned toward his vehicle, Zara swung around too, right into the face of the wind. It caught at her hair, her breath, and a sudden wild gust sent her bike crashing to the ground. Whipping back around, she bent to pick up the machine but Alex beat her by a second. When she attempted to take over the handlebars, their shoulders and hands grazed with a startling tingle of heat. She didn't meet his eyes as she thanked him. She didn't want to know if he'd felt that unsettling zing too.

Completely inappropriate, Zara thought, kicking at the bike stand. It broke off and clattered to the ground. If the kookaburras hadn't taken off for somewhere more sheltered they'd be laughing their heads off!

"Any other damage?" he asked.

"Only to my mood." She swung her leg over the seat and waited for him to hand over the helmet and gloves he'd retrieved from the ground. Frowning, she watched him wipe the dust from them on his very expensive trousers.

"There's no need to do that," she said, disturbed by the image. *Her* helmet, *his* thigh, way too intimate. "Give it here."

He didn't. He gestured toward the sky. "It's going to storm soon."

Zara tipped back her head. Inspected the clouds that scurried low and swift on the blustery wind. "I think we'd better get out of here while we can."

"On that bike?"

"I live in Melbourne. I'm used to weather."

"This isn't the city. That last stretch of road was tricky enough with four wheels under me." Frowning, he tapped her helmet against his thigh. "Perhaps you'd better take shelter inside until it passes."

"Oh, no." Zara shook her head. "I can't stay. I have to get home."

He stared at her a second, his expression unreadable. "In that case, you'd better ride with me."

"What about my bike? It's my only transportation. I can't leave it here."

"I'll send someone to pick it up for you."

Just like that, snap of the fingers, problem solved. Zara couldn't imagine living in a world like that. She huffed out a disbelieving breath. "I don't know if I want—"

"To be stranded here when this storm breaks?"

No, that wasn't what she'd been going to say, but he raised a good point. A point that rippled through her like quicksilver as their gazes locked. No, she did not want to be stranded here, alone, in an isolated cabin, with this man and his cold and hot eyes.

"All right," she relented. "I'll just put my bike inside, out of the weather."

"Pleased to see you can be reasonable."

"When I want to, I can be very reasonable," she countered smoothly, echoing his words and his tone from earlier. She thought about mentioning her real motivation for conceding—she wanted to be there if he found Susannah, to intercede if necessary, to ensure he didn't sway Suse's judgment but decided to keep quiet. She didn't think Alex Carlisle would approve.

Alex didn't want her in his car, but what could he do? The wind continued to gather fury with every passing mile, gusting in uneven spurts that rocked the vehicle and dashed their path with debris. Brought up in the outback, he'd driven in worse weather, but not on roads this tortuous. He'd had to offer her a lift, and now he had to endure all that entailed.

With Zara Lovett, that was one hell of a lot.

Why hadn't someone—Susannah, Emilio, *anyone*— warned him about the legs? A million miles long and snugged in black leather, they'd catch a monk's attention. Alex was not a monk.

Eyes focused on the road, he didn't have to look sideways to picture her in the passenger seat. Her hair a spill of honeyed silk. Whiskey eyes that stretched long and exotic beneath dramatic dark brows. Face too long, nose too big, mouth too wide, she was more about impact than beauty.

Yet he'd taken one look at those long limbs and irregular features and felt a jolt of sexual energy that rocked him to the bone.

He heard her shift in the passenger seat, heard the click of studs and the long metallic whirr of a zip coming undone. Her jacket. He didn't want her taking the damn thing off. He didn't need to know what lay underneath.

Anticipation thickened the air in his lungs. Tension thickened the blood in his veins. He waited…and she settled back into her seat with a soft sigh. With her jacket still on.

What was he doing looking, noticing, responding like a horny teenager? She was Susannah's friend, for Pete's sake.

She shifted again, lifted a hand to comb back her hair, and he caught the drift of her scent, part woman, part leather, part something else he couldn't get a grip of. And he couldn't help wondering how she and Susannah came to be such close friends. They were so unalike, so unlikely.

"Is this your—"

"How did you—"

They'd both started to speak at once, both stopped at the same instant. She waved a hand and said, "You first."

"I was going to ask how you and Susannah became friends." He cut her a sideways look. "You're not what I would have expected."

Turning slightly in her seat, she looked right at him. Raised her brows. "Because I'm wearing leather? Because I ride a bike?"

Point taken. "How long have you been a biker?"

"A biker?" She laughed, a husky draft of amusement that did nothing to ease the awareness in Alex's blood. "I'm not even a wannabe. I ride a bike because it's practical and cheap. Besides, mine's too small."

"That matters?"

"You're asking if size matters?"

He heard the hint of teasing in her voice and resisted the urge to play the game. Not with this woman, not today. "You're telling me with bikes it does."

"Oh, yeah. You need to be riding something called a Dominator or a Monster to call yourself a biker."

"You look the part."

"The leathers? They're for safety, mostly. I like the idea of that layer between me and the bitumen."

"I prefer the idea of a layer of metal."

"Valid point," she conceded, and he sensed her eyes on him. Sensed a new level of interest, a new sharpness in her gaze. "Although those layers of metal don't help you get ahead in traffic jams."

"You still have to stop at the lights," he pointed out. Enjoying the banter, enjoying her eyes on him. "In my car, I can make a phone call, dictate some notes."

"I can study on my bike."

Study? This he couldn't resist. "What do you study?"

"At the lights? Something I've learned by rote. Like anatomy."

"The ankle bone's connected to the calf bone?"

He cut her a quick glance and saw that her smile was as big as the rest of her and packed the same level of impact. "Something like that."

"You're studying medicine?"

"Yup. Third year."

"Dr. Lovett," he mused.

"Okay, okay." She probably rolled her eyes—there was that in her voice—although with his attention back on the road, Alex didn't see the gesture. "I've heard it all before."

He bet she had. And the thought of a bunch of smart-mouth medical students ribbing her with "love-it" gags disturbed him on some primal level.

"You and Susannah," he began, linking their names, reminding himself who she was, why he had no business letting her disturb him in any way. Reminding her that she'd not yet answered his question about their friendship.

"We've been friends for years," she said.

"You were at school together?"

"No."

She didn't elaborate and he needed to concentrate on a tricky section of road. The car rocked hard in the wind and he eased off the gas.

"It's getting wild out there. I'm glad I'm not on my bike." As if to punctuate her words, a sizable branch flew into their path. Then, caught in the wind's bluster, it was gone. He sped up a little, accelerating out of a curve and—

"Look out!"

He saw the fallen tree that blocked the road in the same instant that she gasped the warning. Too late to avoid, but not too late to lessen the inevitable impact. Braking hard, he battled to direct the slewing car away from the thick hardwood trunk, battled to regain control when the tires lost traction and they started a slow-motion sideways slide.

Two

Half expecting air bags to deploy all around her, Zara remained braced with her eyes squeezed shut long after the car slid to a final tree-assisted halt. Apparently they hadn't hit hard enough because nothing happened. Nothing except a hissing fizz from under the hood and what sounded like the thump of a fisted hand against the steering wheel.

A second later his seat belt clicked undone.

"Are you all right?"

The tight note in his voice hinted at concern, and it brought an ache to the back of Zara's eyes that felt very much like tears. Delayed reaction, she diagnosed, since she did not do tears. Slowly she opened her eyes. "I will be."

"Are you sure?"

She managed a faint smile. "Just give me a minute."

She saw his brief hesitation before he attempted to open his door. Without success. His side of the car was jammed against the hefty branches that had halted their progress, and although he applied his shoulder to the door, the only result was an earsplitting wrench of timber against metal.

"I'll need to get out on your side," he said matter-of-factly, and Zara snapped to attention, opening her door and sliding out. The wind lashed at her hair and her unzipped jacket but she paid little heed. Her gaze had fixed on the unscathed panels on her side of the car, still gleaming despite the murky light.

Unmarked because the man currently maneuvering his body across the central console and out the passenger side hadn't panicked. He'd calmly controlled the car's slide. To protect her? That notion weaved a disquieting path through her consciousness and played games with her emotional stability.

To protect them both, she reminded herself. Nothing personal. Nothing to get unsettled and prickly throated about.

Straightening her shoulders, she followed him up front to see the real damage. The car had come to rest bumper-deep in the tree's dense foliage. One jutting branch, it seemed, had pierced the grill and the radiator still hissed its pained response.

She rested a consoling hand on the hood. "Doesn't look as if we'll be going any further. At least, not in this car."

"It could have been a lot worse," he said with a quiet intensity that brought her eyes around to meet his. "I'm rather glad you were in the car."

And not on her bike, without the protection of these sturdy metal panels.

The intensity of his look, of his unspoken message, pounded so powerfully in her chest that she had to look away. To gather her defenses with several deep breaths before she could speak. "It would have been a lot worse but for your quick reflexes."

"I didn't fancy going head-to-head with that piece of lumber." He indicated the bulk of the trunk with a brief nod, and then turned toward the towering forest that edged the road. "Or any of its mates."

She watched him walk back down the road, hands on hips, and knew he'd be reaching the same conclusion she'd just worked her way around to. This back road saw little traffic. They could wait days and not see another vehicle.

"How far to the cabin, do you think?" she asked slowly. At least the cabin had her bike, wheels they could use to get back to civilization.

"Seven miles. A decent walk."

The wind gusted up again, whipping at his suit jacket and bringing up goose bumps on Zara's bare stomach. She cast a quick glance at the sky, at the lowering ceiling of gray, and sucked in a breath thick with the scent of eucalyptus and imminent rain.

"If we don't want to get wet," she said briskly, turning back to the car to fetch her backpack, "we might want to make that a decent run."

They started out at a walk, but with the threat of a cloud-burst hanging over their heads—literally—they picked up the pace after the first mile, despite the flinty ground that shifted underfoot and despite Alex's footwear. Zara listened to those leather soles, designed for nothing more vigorous that stalking the corridors of business power, striking out a solid beat at her side.

As luck would have it, she'd pulled on her leathers over shorts and a workout top before leaving the city. Now those leathers, and his suit jacket and tie, were in her backpack. The biker boots she'd swapped for joggers but he kept up easily, his breathing measured.

Somehow she wasn't surprised. Alex Carlisle looked like a man who took everything in his long, capable stride.

She stepped up the pace again. He, naturally, kept up. From the corner of her eye she caught the easy swing of his arms, bare and tanned beneath rolled-up shirtsleeves, and her chest tightened from more than the aerobic workout.

It mystified her, the intensity and immediacy of this attraction. Sure, he was good-looking. Sure, he oozed testosterone. But she dealt with such men on a daily basis in her work. Beneath the five-thousand-dollar suits they were all just flesh-and-blood men. Not a single one affected her like this.

Why Alex Carlisle?

Because she couldn't have him? Or because she sensed a multitude of layers beneath the expensive veneer and the buff body?

In ten minutes or so they would arrive back at an empty, isolated cabin. This storm might well prevent them from leaving and they would be alone, together. That knowledge jittered through her senses, drove her to run even harder, but she couldn't outrun the man at her side or her extreme awareness of him.

Nor could she outrun the weather.

The sky broke without warning, releasing a short burst of rain that lasted only long enough to soak her to the skin. Then it turned to icy sleet. Head down for protection from the biting wind-driven slush, she might have run right by the turn into the driveway if Alex hadn't called out her name, bringing her head up and around.

At first all she saw was the man stopped by the half-secreted entrance, his dark hair whipped into disarray, his soaked shirt clinging to the hard planes of his torso. A man whose chest worked noticeably with each breath but who still managed to say in a perfectly even voice, "I don't know your plans, but this is as far as I'm going."

Zara shoved a dripping hank of hair back from her face. "I was thinking of going around the block again," she managed to gasp. "But if you've had enough, let's call it quits."

Zara had stayed at the cabin enough times to know what to expect. One room, one bed, one outside bathroom. No electricity, no hot water, no neighbors. One key hidden in the same spot behind the wood box on the porch.

Three-quarters of an hour after Alex took the key from her useless, numb fingers to open the door, Zara thought she might have stopped shivering. Finally. The fire he'd patiently built and nurtured from damp kindling into a blazing inferno helped. So had losing her wet clothes and wrapping herself snugly in one of the pair of thick sleeping bags Alex had found.

Draped over the handlebars of her bike and a chair he'd dragged fireside, her thin gym clothes would soon be dry. So would his shirt, which meant she could stop *not* watching him prowl around the cabin, all bare-chested and beautiful in the rusty firelight. She'd decided it was much safer and more relaxing to watch the flames flicker and dance over the logs in the fireplace.

Sitting cross-legged inside her downy cocoon, staring into the blaze, she could even put a positive spin to this misadventure. With Alex isolated out here, Susannah had more time to think—or to get wherever she'd gone to do that thinking—without him turning up to influence her decision. Zara might be stormbound with a man who stirred her libido in all kinds of forbidden ways, but she had willpower. She knew what she could have and what was off-limits. Take chocolate, for example…

Bad example.

With a wry grimace, she pressed a hand to her empty stomach. Thinking about food reminded her of how little she'd eaten today and how little Alex had found in his preliminary investigation of the cabin. Two pillows, two sleeping bags, two kerosene lamps, no kerosene. One box of matches.

Right now she could hear him executing a more thorough search of the kitchen cupboards.

"Any luck?" she asked hopefully, when the sounds of doors opening and shutting ceased.

"Unless there's something edible in the first-aid kit, we're dead out of luck."

She turned then to find him leaning back against what passed for a kitchen bench. And for the first time since they'd walked through the door, for the first time since he'd ordered her out of her wet clothes, since he'd busied himself with building the fire and setting their clothes out to dry, he met her eyes.

Nice that it was across the width of the cabin. Nice that the distance and the shadowy light disguised the hot lick of reaction in her eyes, in her blood, in her bare-naked skin beneath the silky lining of the sleeping bag. She wrapped it more securely around her shoulders and attempted to relax. They were stuck with each other for the duration of the storm; why not make it as easy and comfortable as possible?

"Not even an out-of-date can of beans?" she asked.

"Sadly, no."

"You know what's really sad? I stopped on my way out here for fuel and what was allegedly lunch. At the time I thought I was doing myself a favor not eating it!"

"You didn't save the leftovers?"

Zara chuckled at his hopeful tone. "No, although that's not the saddest bit. In a moment of weakness I almost bought a couple of chocolate bars, you know, for later. But I resisted."

"Damn."

"You like chocolate?"

"Like is perhaps too mild a word," he said with a slow smile. "It's my sin of choice."

Standing there in the shadows with his bare chest and flat abdomen and low-riding trousers, with that deadly little smile exaggerating the sensual bow of his top lip and deepening the grooves in his lean cheeks, he looked like a different kind of sinner. And a different kind of sin.

Temptation snaked through Zara's veins, the dark, rich, sumptuous chocolate kind. Temptation to ask how often he sinned, to suggest it had done him no harm, to ask about his second choice. To flirt and indulge herself for once while she stripped away the veneer to the man beneath.

She didn't. She couldn't. He was Susannah's.

"I resisted the siren call." Zara shrugged, a silky slide of her bare shoulders inside the sleeping bag. "It's not been one of my better days for choices."

"I don't suppose it worked out quite the way you planned when you got up this morning."

"We have that in common," she said, and regretted her candor instantly. The mood changed, grew thick and weighty with the reminder of how his day had started and what had brought them together. His wedding. Her worry.

"Why did you disapprove of me marrying Susannah?" he asked.

Zara exhaled slowly. So much for the easy banter. So much for comfortable. She felt the tension in his gaze, in her limbs, and concentrated on how to answer.

In truth, Susannah hadn't told her much about her relationship with Alex Carlisle and that was the problem. If Zara ever fell in love, she couldn't imagine clamming up on her best friend in their regular e-mail or IM or phone updates. She'd have sung it, laughed it, lived it, breathed it. Susannah hadn't. Sure, she'd mentioned meeting Alex and going out with him a couple of times, then the next thing Zara knew, she'd agreed to marry him.

"I wouldn't have disapproved," she said slowly, "if Susannah had appeared more enthusiastic about her wedding."

"She wasn't happy?"

"You're asking me?"

The line of his surprisingly full lips tightened. "We haven't spent a lot of time together, not since she moved back to Melbourne."

"You spent last weekend together," Zara pointed out. They'd flown to his family's outback station so Susannah could meet his mother and apparently there'd been a small engagement party. "Didn't you notice anything the matter?"

Heck, Zara had only seen her friend twice during the last week and *she'd* noticed her quietness, her distraction. That's why she'd prodded her at dinner last night. That's why she'd asked if Susannah was very, very sure.

Obviously her fiancé hadn't noticed. He stood in stony-faced silence for at least another minute before he asked, "Is there someone else?"

Even across the room and through the deepening twilight she could see the stormy tension in his eyes. The breath caught hard in her chest and she had to look away. Had to force her focus to that bolt-from-the-blue question. Something had definitely been going on with Susannah this last week, but another man? It seemed so unlikely that

Zara hadn't even considered the possibility. She did so now, for a long intense moment.

Perhaps she'd needed someone who gave her more time and consideration. Zara could believe that. But she couldn't believe that Susannah would cheat.

"No." She shook her head. "Not when she'd agreed to marry you."

The moment spun out, taut and silent but for the whistling howl of the wind and the intermittent crack and spit of the fire. She didn't know if he believed her, couldn't tell what he was thinking.

"What will you do now?" she asked.

"What can I do?" He pushed away from the bench. "For now we're stuck here with nothing to do but wait out the storm."

All matter-of-fact, all purpose, he crossed the room toward her and Zara jerked up straighter, eyes wide and mouth turning dry. But he skirted around to the side of the hearth, then squatted down to feed the fire with another chunk of wood. She tried to look away, some place where the revitalized leap of flames didn't limn the hard planes of his torso in golden light. Where she didn't notice how his midnight-dark hair had dried thick and wavy and ruffled, or how her fingers curled with a need to reach out and touch.

Zara swallowed and discovered that her throat was as dry as her mouth. She wriggled an arm free of her cocoon and reached for her water. She took a long swig and offered him the bottle. Then watched him drink, watched the slide of his throat as he swallowed.

Oh, gads. She had to stop doing that. Watching him. Staring.

"That's a first-rate fire," she said, turning to stare fixedly into the blaze instead. "Were you a Boy Scout?"

"Me?" He snorted softly. "No way."

"Not the Carlisle way?"

"I grew up in the outback, Zara, on a cattle station. No Boy Scouts out there."

"But plenty of fires?" She gave up and turned her curious gaze his way. Still too attractive—far too attractive, squatting there by the hearth, one hand holding a solid fire iron in a loose grip, turning it over and over in a slow, measured motion.

"The campfire was one of our first lessons, the first year we were allowed out on a muster."

"You mustered cattle?"

He huffed out a soft sound. "Is that so hard to imagine?"

So, okay, she'd known the Carlisles owned oodles of cattle country up in the north—the tabloids loved to refer to the brothers as "Princes of the Outback"—but she'd never pictured them taking an active role. If she'd pictured them at all. Now the figure of Alex the cowboy rode into her imagination, and strangely she didn't laugh. An hour or two back she would have.

Another layer peeled away, revealed, disturbing.

"How about you, Zara?" he asked, poking at the fire now. "Were you a Girl Scout?"

She smiled, despite her unsettling thoughts. "No. Obviously I wasn't."

"You like the bush, though?"

"How did you know that?"

"You said you like coming up here."

Ah, right, so she had. Earlier, out on the porch. When she'd been ferreting out the key with her frozen fingers. "Here it's like each day stretches ahead with all these hours and the freedom to do whatever I want with them. No pressure, no timetable."

"You don't mind the lack of amenities?"

"No." She smiled and shook her head. "And that's a straight-out lie. I do miss a decent shower. Steamy. Hot. Indecently long."

She finished on a husky note of yearning and looked up to find him watching her, his eyes so still and intent that she felt a hot, liquid curl in her belly. A chocolate response, she thought. Rich and sweet and tempting at the moment, but sinfully bad for her body in the long run.

"Do you come here alone?"

"Look around, Alex." She looked at the one bed and her pulse fluttered. "This is hardly the place for a group getaway."

"I wasn't talking about a group." No, she could tell he was talking about a man. About hot and steamy, one-on-one getaways. And if he weren't watching her with those deeply shadowed eyes, if she weren't sitting here naked with her sinfully chocolate thoughts, she would have laughed out loud.

She didn't.

"I come here when I want to be alone, to escape," she explained softly.

The fire crackled and hissed, the only sound for a long time. Until he asked, "What do you need to escape from, Zara? When you come up here?"

"Life. Schedules. Busy, busy, busy." She shrugged. Kept on talking when she probably should have shut up. "The last time was after my mother passed away and I was trying to escape the…" She paused, frowning as she tried to find the words to explain how she'd felt, the emptiness, the knowledge that she was all alone in the world. No family, no connections. "This might sound weird, but I was trying to escape the aloneness. Up here that's okay, but not at home. Not in the house where there'd always been us."

"Only the two of you?"

"Yes."

"I'm sorry about your mother," he said softly, after a pause. "Was this long ago?"

"Three years." Sometimes it felt longer. Other times she could picture her mum so vividly, hear her voice so clearly, Ginger might have been sitting at Zara's side, nudging her with an elbow, making her laugh at a witty observation on the world. Or on the men who ran the world.

She had been some cynic, her mum, the ex-stripper!

"You have good memories?"

"Oh, about a ton of them." She started to smile, but then her gaze snared with his and her pulse flickered and leaped like the flames in the fireplace. Like the flames reflected in his eyes.

For a long moment—too long—she couldn't look away, couldn't smile, could barely breathe. She recognized the danger in the moment. Knew her emotions, her heart, her soul were laid open and wanting by memories of her mum. And just when she thought he might say something he shouldn't, something dangerous and inadvisable, a log snapped and broke in a shower of sparks.

Alex reacted instantly, swearing roundly as he jumped to his feet. Zara couldn't contain the bubble of laughter, born partly of tension released and partly of the sight of him swatting at his trousers where the hot embers had hit.

Hunkered down, as he'd been, that was a rather delicate spot.

He shot her a filthy look. "I'm glad you find this amusing."

"Better you than me," she said, grinning. Until his expression changed and she knew he visualized her jumping about swatting at her slithery covering. Or her jumping about without the slithery covering.

"Yeah," he said softly, seeing she'd got the message. "Exactly."

And he turned back to the fire, squatting down again to poke the burning logs into submission with a fiercer than necessary hand. Despite the previous moment, she couldn't help smiling at his take-that brand of vengeance. So very un-prince-like, so very male.

"Lucky you didn't take my advice before," she said.

He paused in his energetic fire-taming to cut her a questioning look.

"When I suggested you should take your wet trousers off."

He huffed out a half laugh and muttered something that sounded like, "Self-preservation."

"You had a premonition that the fire might attack?"

He put down the tool with what looked like slow and deliberate care. Then he stood in the same measured way, and looked down at her with unflinching directness. "No. I thought one of us bare-assed was more than enough."

Zara swallowed. She hadn't expected such a forthright admission, such forthright language, or to find this new layer he'd revealed so deadly attractive. So insidiously tempting. *No, no, no.* She swallowed again and pushed that chocolate-coated temptation right to the back of her mind.

"My clothes—" Dipping her head in that direction, she tucked her legs underneath her, preparing to stand. "They should be almost dry."

Since he wasn't trussed up like a mummy, Alex got to her things first…which wouldn't have been so bad if the clothes were, say, like his shirt. Or his suit jacket or her leather jeans and jacket or even her shorts.

But, no, by the time she'd struggled to her feet, by the time she'd shuffled to his side and freed a hand, by the time she'd said, "Here, let me get them," he was holding her underwear.

Her panties to be exact. And, okay, they weren't violet lace or a scarlet G-string or anything remotely racy. They were just your practical, black, boy-leg hipsters prettied up with a pink bunny-ears appliqué. But they were in his hand and that felt incredibly intimate. The way his thumb stroked over the satin bunny ears and onto the cotton even more so.

"They appear to be dry."

"Then I'd best put them on," she managed to say, low, husky, *bad*. "Self-preservation, you know."

His nostrils flared slightly. His eyes darkened with heat and knowledge and approval, but then he shook his head as if to clear it and pushed the panties into her hand. Closed her fingers around the soft fabric with the insistent pressure of his own. And the combination of that slightly rough-textured touch and the rueful note to his final words held her rooted to the spot long after he'd walked away. Long after he'd walked out into the cold, wet twilight and closed the door behind him.

"You'd best put on everything you can find, Zara, of yours and mine. If this storm doesn't ease up soon it's going to be a hellishly long night of self-preservation."

Three

Zara dressed quickly, although not in everything she could find. Still, her brief athletic top and snug shorts seemed vastly inadequate. She fingered the sleeve of his shirt and fought the temptation to wrap herself in the fire-warmed fabric. Wrapping herself in anything that smelled of Alex Carlisle's expensive blend of man and cologne would not do her any favors.

She let go of the sleeve and reached for her jacket instead. The leather jeans, however, were too much. A minute after pulling them on, her skin felt clammy and uncomfortable. She unzipped her jacket, she moved away from the fire. Pressing her cheek against the cool glass of a window helped marginally but in the end she took the jeans off.

Self-preservation be damned. Nothing was going to happen between them, whether they were here all night or not. Nothing was going to happen because neither of them wanted it to, right?

"Right," she affirmed.

But when she pressed her face back against the window-pane, the hot-cold contrast sent a shiver of reaction through her flesh. She leaned closer to the glass and listened to the elevated thud of her heart. That, she acknowledged, had nothing at all to do with the roaring fire.

Outside, the wind drove intermittent blasts of rain hard against the log walls of the cabin and slapped wet gum branches over the corrugated iron of the outhouse roof. Alex stood in the sheltering lee of the porch and considered his options. One insistent side of his brain wanted to keep on walking, out where the icy squall might cool the heat in his skin and his blood. The other side asked what good a chill would do when the fever's source lay inside his pants.

Or inside the four sturdy walls of the cabin.

Zara Lovett with her whiskey eyes and husky laugh and steady I've-got-your-measure gaze. Zara Lovett who'd strode into his life on killer legs and lit a powder keg in his gut.

Chemistry. The kind of powerful, explosive mix Alex made a habit of avoiding. He didn't like fireworks. They reminded him of his birth father's fierce temper, of the heat he feared in his own nature, of the passion he'd worked long and hard to control.

He liked smooth and easy. He liked stability. He liked his relationship with Susannah for those very reasons.

Nothing had changed in the last six hours. He still needed to satisfy the terms of his father's will; he still wanted that within the confines of a stable relationship. A marriage to the right woman. One with the same goals and beliefs, the same background and values. One who respected the time and energy he spent on his career and who didn't demand any more than he could give.

Nothing had changed. Just because he'd crossed paths with a golden-haired beauty who made his male glands jump to attention didn't mean things would change. Once the storm cleared he would ride out of here and find Susannah and convince her all over again that they had the goods to make a marriage work.

That was his goal. That was his duty. That was what mattered. Alex set his expression to match his mindset and went back inside.

Eventually Zara gave up the pretense of ignoring him. What was the point? She'd accepted that nothing was going to happen between them and since he'd returned from outside he'd given off the same vibes.

Why not enjoy the only available form of entertainment? He was, after all, eminently watchable.

So, she'd watched him mess with the fire, watched him fetch more wood, watched him build neat symmetrical stacks beside the hearth as if rationing the supply for the hours ahead. He'd even fiddled with the broken stand on her bike, until she'd forced him to acknowledge that he couldn't fix it without a welder.

Alex Carlisle was hot, but not that hot.

For the past ten minutes she'd watched him pace, appreciating the way he moved and the muscular definition of his deltoids, his pectorals, his biceps. Obviously he worked out. Obviously he wasn't used to doing nothing.

"You're not used to having all this time on your hands, are you?"

He answered with a soft grunt of assent, essentially male, ridiculously attractive.

Zara hadn't moved far from the window, but now she leaned back against the wall and crossed her arms over her chest. "What would you be doing if we weren't stuck here?"

He stopped pacing, turned slowly and stared at her. "You mean tonight?"

His wedding night.

That significance struck her in a wave of hot-cold shock. She thought about grabbing one of her joggers—no, better make it one of her biker boots!—and shoving it in her mouth.

"How much detail do you require?" he asked with a surprisingly wry cut to his mouth. So, okay, it didn't quite make up for the dark heat in his eyes and the flare of response in her body, but she could play along with it. She could pretend she didn't notice. And if she kept on talking, maybe she could distract herself from further wedding-night imaginings.

"I meant some other night. An average night."

"I'd be working."

"Even on a Saturday?"

"Possibly." He shrugged as if the day of the week made no difference. "Depends where I am, what I'm working on. Whether there's a function I'm obligated to attend."

Obligated. What an interesting slant on social life. Not that she had a social life, but still… "No wild rave parties then?"

His lips quirked. "Not that I can recall."

"Why do you work so hard?" she asked after another moment. A moment of watching him snag his shirt from the back of the chair, of feeling the skim of sensation in her own skin as he pulled it on. Of forcing herself to say something, anything, to distract her from the thick beat of awareness in her blood.

He gave a loose-muscled shrug, one that punctuated his next words perfectly. "It's what I do."

"Work is your life then?"

"Is that a bad thing?"

"Not at all," she said quickly. "I'm pretty much the same. Dedicated—" she almost said "married," but rectified that at the last second "—to my work."

"Your dedication shows," he said slowly and she frowned, not understanding how her dedication to medical studies would show. "Your fitness," he clarified.

Ah, he was talking about the run back to the cabin. "You didn't do so badly yourself. For a desk jockey."

"Surprised I kept up?"

Zara met his eyes and smiled. "You were wearing a business suit and leather loafers. You had no business keeping up!"

"Will it make you feel any better to know I'm suffering for that now?"

For a second she became a little lost in the shadowy hint of his smile, in the delicious energy that seemed to pump between them, and then she got his meaning. Her nose wrinkled in sympathy. "Blisters?"

"A couple." His shrug was a bit tight and she figured he was uncomfortable drawing attention to anything less than a broken bone or dislocated joint. He was, after all, a man. That was something you tended to notice about Alex Carlisle.

Pivoting off her leaning post, she headed toward the cupboards. "I'll get the first-aid kit."

"It's only a couple of blisters."

Which Zara preferred to see for herself. She retrieved the kit and marched over to the chair near the fire. "Step into my consulting room and I'll take a look."

"Forget it, Zara."

"I'm training to be a doctor. I need practical experience."

"I'm sure you do," Alex said, not moving a muscle. "But you're not getting that hands-on training with me."

It took a moment, but then she got the veiled meaning in his words. He saw the little jolt of reaction, the flicker of her gaze from him to the chair and back again. He knew she'd caught a glimpse of the picture slow-burning through his brain.

Him sitting on the chair. Her kneeling at his feet, her head bent so her long hair swung loose and honey-gold in the firelight. Close enough that it brushed and snagged against the dark cloth of his trousers.

She got that he was talking about self-preservation again.

The knowledge flashed in her eyes, softened her lips, grabbed him by the throat with soft female teeth and growled in his most masculine parts. Just the image of her kneeling at his feet. He hadn't even reached the part where she placed his foot on the smooth stretch of her bare thigh.

Hell.

A couple of minutes ago they'd been talking, just talking. How did they get to this point? The point where he felt he might have to walk out into that icy slash of rain. He crossed the room, turned, paced back. They'd started out talking about what they'd normally be doing on an average night.

"You haven't told me—" he stopped and looked at her again, sitting by the fire, the first-aid kit open in her hands "—how you spend your nights."

Carefully she closed the lid and set the box aside. "Mostly I'm studying."

"You can't study all the time. What do you do to relax and take your mind off the books?"

"I visit with friends. Or listen to music. Sometimes I knit."

That tickled him. The image of this earthy, sexy, physical woman involved in such a restful, old-fashioned craft. "You knit."

Defensiveness drew her brows into a solid dark frown. "Is that a bad thing?"

"No. Just…unexpected. Did you learn from your mother? Your grandmother? Great-aunt Mable?"

She smiled. "My mother, in a roundabout way. When Mum was sick, the occupational therapist taught her and I learned as well. You kind of get addicted to the click of the needles and to watching the piece grow. Linda says—" She drew up short and expelled a breath. "You don't need to hear about this."

"No, but I'd like to."

She gave him a come-on-honestly look and he waited, patiently, until she shook her head and continued. "Linda, the therapist, says the key with knitting is that you're usually making a gift for someone else. Part of the therapeutic deal is that while you knit you're thinking about the person you're knitting for. Usually that's someone you care about so that adds to the positive vibes. Anyway, that's her theory."

"What does the doctor in training say about that theory?"

"Anything relaxing is good for a body." She looked up at him with a deprecating smile. "So, yeah, I knit. There it is—my Saturday-night confession."

"Not much of a sin."

"No." Her answer had a husky edge, and the notion of sin lingered in its aftermath and stretched the moment with dangerous tension. "Is chocolate your only obsession?"

"There's also the horses."

"As in horse racing? You gamble?"

He took that note of disbelief as a compliment and smiled. "No, that would be my brother Rafe. I race them. I study form and breeding. I can be obsessive."

"I imagine so."

Alex thought he could easily obsess about that husky register of her voice. That particular look in her eyes, part heat, part curiosity. The beauty spot below her left cheekbone that his gaze kept sliding back to, and the long, smooth length of her legs wrapped around his hips while she took him into her body.

"Do you breed your racehorses?"

It took a second to get past the hard hum of lust in his ears and really hear the question. To form an appropriate answer. "I have an interest in several stallions."

"Intriguing," she said slowly. But the change in her expression wasn't curiosity. It was a cooling, a withdrawal, and he had to know what that was about. Had to know what was ticking away in that sharp brain of hers.

"Intriguing...how?"

"I just remembered something Susannah told me. A thought I had at the time."

"Come on, Zara. You can't leave that hanging."

She eyed him speculatively for a beat. "You might prefer that I did."

"Do I look like someone who can't handle plain-speak?"

"Okay," she said, holding his gaze, accepting his challenge to speak her mind. "When Susannah told me why you needed to marry so quickly, when she told me why you'd chosen her, it put me in mind of a stud-breeding enterprise. I thought, this Alex Carlisle has studied the pedigrees. He's decided that the Horton and Carlisle genotypes would meld nicely."

Alex stared at her narrowly. Where the hell had that come from? "What," he asked slowly, "did Susannah tell you?"

"That you and your brothers won't inherit your father's estate unless one of you produces a baby. Which, I'm sorry, sounds like a disgustingly commercial reason for breeding a baby. I mean, don't you have enough of everything already? Do you really need more money?"

"How do you know it's about money? Did you ask Susannah? Did you ask me?"

She closed her mouth on whatever else she'd been about to say. He should have done the same. Her opinion of him shouldn't matter. Her words shouldn't seethe through him like a wash of acid.

"I owe Charles Carlisle for everything I have, everything I am. His last wish was a grandchild for my mother, and what we're doing—what *I'm* doing—" he tapped two fingers against his chest "—is honoring that wish. It's not about any inheritance. It's about repaying my stepfather. It's about family."

Renewed rain struck a staccato beat against the iron roof. Loud enough to mask the crackle of firewood, not loud enough to drown out the heavy thud of his heartbeat or the screaming knowledge that he'd said too much. Revealed too much of himself, of the passion at his heart, of emotions that showed vulnerability.

"I'm sorry I said what I did. That was unfair," she conceded after a long moment. But then she lifted her chin with a hint of defiance. "I was right in saying you selected Susannah though, wasn't I? You were looking for a mother for this child, and you cast around for the ideal candidate."

"You don't think she'll make a good mother?"

"She will make a splendid mother, but that's not what I asked." She huffed out an exasperated breath, then rose to her feet. "Why did you ask her to marry you? Why didn't you just offer a business deal and benefits for the child, without the marriage?"

"I believe a child deserves a stable, happy, two-parent home."

"That is so old-fashioned! Don't you think a child is better with one parent who loves and cares than in an unhappy home? Look at me." Eyes glittering with a passionate heat, she moved closer. "I'm the role model for a single-parent family. I never needed a father who didn't care about me wandering around the periphery of my life. Or in and out of it according to his whim."

Alex's gaze narrowed. "Is that what your father did?"

"Hell, no! I didn't even know who he was until just before Mum died. I tried to meet him and he didn't want to know me."

"And what if he had?" he asked, turning her argument around on her. "Would you have enjoyed joint custody arrangements? Being shunted from one house to the other?"

She hitched her chin even higher. "No, but that doesn't make a child the right reason to marry."

"What *is* the right reason to marry?"

"Love," she said without hesitation. "Falling madly for someone you want to share your whole life with. Someone who makes your heart warm just looking at him. Someone you can't bear living without."

"I didn't pick you for a romantic." Alex shook his head slowly. Then he moved a step closer, captured her gaze with the steady intensity of his as he bent closer. "So, if you were to meet someone tomorrow who made your blood hot just looking at him. If you fell madly in love and wanted to share your life with this man, you'd marry him?"

For an instant she seemed absorbed in the moment, in his eyes, in whatever the hell he thought he was trying to prove. Then some kind of resolve snapped in her eyes and she stepped away from him and the blazing intensity of that moment.

"Tomorrow?" She turned with her back to the fire and

gave a casual shrug. "No. I can't afford a relationship of any sort until I finish my studies and establish a career."

"Can't afford?"

"The time, the commitment." Laughing softly, she shook her head. "Between study and my job I don't have time to date."

"Your course is that full on?"

"Oh, yeah. And I need to maintain my grades. I'm shooting for an honors year in medical science next year." Her eyes burned with a different kind of intensity, something from within that caught at his gut in a way nothing about her had before. But then her lips curled with a curious wryness. "Plus, I promised my mother I'd get my degree."

"To make her proud?"

"Oh, I'm pretty sure she'd be proud of me with or without the degree," she said with quiet confidence. "But I deferred my studies to nurse her and she made me promise I'd go back. It would have broken her heart if I hadn't."

In the ensuing silence Alex realized that the rain had stopped, at least for now. The only sound was the crackle of firewood…that and a silence so tense that it might have crackled as well. And through that moment, he had to force himself to remain still. Not to reach out and touch her in some way. That, he knew, would be a step he couldn't take back.

"The rain's stopped." Inconsequential, but he had to say something. The silence was stretching into awkwardness, as if they both acknowledged revealing too much, too soon. The hush of darkness was falling over the cabin, too, and with it the knowledge of a decision to be made. To leave or to stay.

Her eyes met his with that same jitter of knowledge. "Are you thinking about leaving?"

"Not yet. The wind hasn't died down much. I'll give it a while."

"It might keep blowing all night."

"It might."

She seemed to give that ordinary answer an inordinate amount of consideration. She rolled her shoulders and tucked her hands into the pockets of her jacket. Moistened the full curve of her lips. "We probably should just give in to the weather and stay the night."

"Earlier you said you had to get home."

"To study."

"Is there anyone going to worry when you don't come home?"

"I have a housemate. Tim, who you spoke to. He'll wonder but he'll likely think I decided to stay up here the night. He knows I love this place."

"Staying would be sensible," he agreed, eyes still holding hers, body entertaining all manner of non-sensible ideas. "You can have the bed."

"That wouldn't be fair. I think—"

"Don't suggest we share, Zara," he interrupted. "Because *that* wouldn't be fair."

She didn't argue. They didn't have to discuss why, it hummed in the air between them. "I'm just going out," she told him, and he saw the flare of her nostrils as she drew a breath, "to the bathroom."

When she opened the door, the wind rushed in and cut an icy slice right through to his bones. That settled his uneasy mind about their decision to stay, and he set about tending the fire and setting out her sleeping bag on the bed. His on the floor as far away as possible.

And when she returned and started stripping off her jacket, pulling off her shoes, preparing for bed, he escaped to the bathroom. The cold-water shower helped for a while, but only for a while. Then she rolled over in her sleeping bag, and he knew she wasn't asleep and he couldn't control the rush of reaction that burned in his skin.

It was no surprise to find himself painfully hard. Ridiculous. He hadn't felt this out of control of his responses since his first adolescent crush.

Quietly frustrated, unable to sit still, he got up from the fireside and padded to the window. He could no more control the stir of heat in his groin than he could control the unrelenting lash of the storm outside. He felt trapped, not only within these four walls but trapped within his body. His slow exhalation fogged the cold pane of glass and he heard her stir restlessly again on the bed. A hush of movement as quiet as her breathing, and with the howl of the wind and the renewed slice of rain against the glass he shouldn't have heard.

But he did.

He didn't turn. He stood still and alert and erect.

Inconsequentially, he thought that his brothers would get a laugh out of his predicament. Especially Rafe who had a thing about fate and chance and luck. He wouldn't be standing by the window while his body ached for a woman. He'd take this meeting, the storm, the one bed, this amazing sexual fascination, and turn it into a sign.

Alex didn't hold any stock in signs but he did trust logic and gut instinct. Both had told him from the start that Zara wasn't the right woman, not for a man who wanted peace and stability and control. In half a day she'd outrun him and out-thought him, intrigued him and challenged him, made him smile and scowl and ultimately turned him into a victim of his glands.

And the night was only just beginning.

Oh, yeah. Rafe would get a real laugh out of this.

Four

Zara tried every relaxation technique she had learned and employed over the years but all to no avail. An hour or more later, she was no closer to sleep than when she'd crawled into her sleeping bag. Up here she usually slept easily, embraced by the soothing country dark and the earthy scents of pine and eucalyptus and timber. Often she was so worn out by a day spent bush walking or casting a line into one of several trout-rich streams within hiking distance that she fell into an eight-hour stretch of solid, blissful, dream-free slumber.

She probably snored a treat.

A smile touched her lips at the thought, then turned warmly reminiscent as she fixed on the day Susannah flabbergasted her with a lesson in trout fishing. It had been quite the weekend for shocks, starting with the cabin itself. When Susannah invited her away to "a little place my grandfather left me," she'd expected "little place" to be one of those classic understatements the wealthy tended to use.

She hadn't expected anything this basic, rustic, primitive.

And she sure hadn't expected her newly discovered half sister with her cool elegance and private-school accent to display such skill in casting a fishing line. They'd only known each other a couple of months—a couple of awkward, getting-to-know-each-other months because of the circumstances under which they'd met.

Zara, distressed and grief-angry at her mother's failing health, had been on a mission to meet her father. After discovering some clippings among her mother's things, she'd found him easily enough. Susannah had overheard their heated exchange, including her father's callous dismissal of Zara's paternity claim, and sought her out afterward.

She'd wanted to meet her only sibling and to plead with her to keep their relationship secret. "Mother doesn't know about his affairs. She's not well and a shock like this would about kill her."

Zara was happy to oblige. After meeting the coldhearted son of a bitch, she didn't want to acknowledge Edward Horton as her father. It had taken a few coffees, a couple of lunches, several long, bonding conversations about their respective mothers' illnesses and a defining weekend at a mountain cabin to overturn her preconceptions about Susannah.

She was no spoiled society princess, and Zara had felt mean and shamed for making that assumption. Especially when Susannah had told her why she was sharing the line-casting skill. "Pappy Horton taught me to fish. He was a wonderful man, our grandfather. He would have brought you up here and taught you himself, if he'd known about you."

Zara had stared at her with wide, stunned eyes. "Really?"

"That's why I brought you here, sis. I hate being out of

phone coverage. I hate not having a hot shower. But I wanted to share something with you, something of family. Please, use the cabin whenever you like. Pappy would have wanted that."

After that weekend, they'd become firm friends, as close as sisters, although that word had never been spoken again. As much as Zara disliked the lack of acknowledgment, she'd grown to accept it because Susannah was protecting the mother she loved.

The wrong result for the right reason…and that brought her rambling thoughts right back to Alex Carlisle.

She'd prejudged him, the same as she'd done with Susannah. She'd imagined the big man painted in the media, powerful and power hungry, self-important and self-involved. A younger, wealthier version of Edward Horton really, and if that didn't predispose her to dislike him then nothing would!

He'd asked Susannah to marry him—the wrong result—for the best of reasons. Yet she couldn't help feeling he wasn't right for Susannah. Or was she looking for excuses? Justification to stifle the guilty knowledge that she was fiercely attracted to him?

With a frustrated sigh, she flipped onto her back and kicked at the sleeping bag when it didn't turn with her. So, okay, she was attracted. She could be honest about those biochemical reactions in her body, which she couldn't do a thing to control. The isolation didn't help. Being alone with an enormously attractive man, especially after the adrenaline-producing crash and the run back to the cabin, was suggestive.

But nothing was going to happen. Not even if Susannah appeared at the door right now and said, "Go ahead, be my guest, he's all yours!"

She didn't have time for a relationship, not even a brief fling, not with Alex Carlisle. It would be too intense, fierce, hot, consuming. She knew this without question, as surely as she knew where he stood right now, still and silent and watchful.

Watching her.

Physical awareness washed through her body, more potent than anything she'd ever felt. The wind had died down but the rain had started up again, a steady drumming beat on the iron roof that echoed in her body. The heightened beat of her pulse. The restless throb of desire in her veins.

Lying on her back staring up at the faint play of shadow over the darkened ceiling, she should not have known where he stood…or that he stood. She should not have heard him move, either, above the noise of the rain, but she did.

She sat up, found him by the sink, a dark, solid silhouette beyond the low glow cast by the banked fire.

"I was just getting a drink," he said. "Did I wake you?"

Zara shook her head. "No. I've been awake a while. I couldn't sleep."

"Are you cold?"

The husky edge of concern in his voice rolled through her, a shiver that had nothing to do with the cold. "No. Not cold."

Hot, much too hot. And dry, she realized, as she watched the shadow of movement as he lifted an arm to drink the water he'd poured. As she attempted to moisten her mouth.

"I'd love some water, actually." She started to unzip her bag, to swing her legs free.

"Stay there. I'll bring it."

The faucet hissed again as he refilled her bottle from the rainwater tank, then he started toward her and there was an almost expectant hush in her body, a still anticipation as she waited for him to walk from the deep shadows into clearer sight. He wore his trousers and shirt, unbuttoned and hanging loose. A tousled, disreputable version of the polished man who'd climbed from that car six or so hours ago.

He paused beside the bed long enough for Zara to notice, right there at eye height, that several sparks from the fire had burned right through the fine cloth of his trousers. Long enough to see that he wore white underwear. And that both underwear and damaged trousers were distended by the jut of his arousal.

That all swam dizzily before her eyes another second before he sat on the side of the bed. A frown colored his voice as he asked, "Are you all right?" and she opened her eyes and discovered how close he sat.

Her heart thudded. Close, hot, aroused. "Just overheated. And thirsty."

He handed her the bottle. She thanked him politely and lifted it to her lips. Then, as she drank, she made the mistake of meeting his eyes and the burn of heat in their deeply shadowed depths sucked at her breath. And her mouthful of water went down the wrong way, leaving her choking and coughing and disconcerted.

She couldn't meet his eyes. And because she looked away, she had no notice of what he was doing, no warning that he was going to touch her. The pad of his thumb stroked across her chest, spreading dampness against her hot skin.

Air hissed between her teeth, and for a moment she thought that was the sizzle of his touch on her skin. Her eyes shot to his, connected with that same scorch. "What are you doing?"

He took his hand away and disappointment tightened hard and low in her belly.

"Spillage." His gaze slipped down to where he'd touched, then lower. "Best I leave the rest to you."

She looked down too, saw what she hadn't even felt. The damp circle over one half of her breast. The clear outline of her nipple. She swallowed. "The water went down the wrong way."

"I noticed."

Their eyes connected again, with a glint of knowledge at what they'd both noticed. In her, in him.

And before she did something or said something regrettable, she searched around for a safer topic. The first thing her eyes lit upon was his sleeping bag spread on the far side of the fire, on the perimeter of its red-tinged glow. Smooth and untouched. "I know I'm having trouble sleeping," she said, "but it looks like you haven't even tried."

He turned a little, followed her line of gaze. "The floor wasn't so inviting."

"Your choice," she reminded him. "We could be sharing the bed."

Slowly his gaze slid back to hers. Something that looked like *are-you-kidding-me?* crossed his expression and she felt the heat, the color, the knowledge flare below her skin in her throat and her cheeks. But she lifted her chin and met that incredulous look.

"We both have sleeping bags. It's not as if I'm inviting you to slide between the sheets with me." She lifted her shoulders in an attempt at a casual shrug. "We can top and tail if that helps."

"I doubt that would help, Zara."

She inhaled sharply, swamped by the vivid imagery he painted with that one line. With the wry intonation and the burn of heat in eyes she had once thought cold as the winter ocean.

That seemed so very long ago.

"If I trust you," she said, straightening her shoulders and meeting those eyes steadily, "can you agree to trust me?"

"Why would you trust me?" he asked warily.

"Because you're my best friend's fiancé and a gentleman." She paused a beat. "Because we're both adults and neither one of us wants anything to happen between us."

He continued to eye her with a curious mix of circumspection and concentration, as if he were searching back through her words looking for hidden traps. She scooted to the other side of the bed, which, being a double, wasn't a terribly long way.

But it was a stance and a demonstration of intent. *Me on my side, you on yours.* When he still didn't move, she patted the mattress she'd cleared. "Don't be a chicken, Alex. Get your pillow and sleeping bag and give it a try. "

The coward taunt worked. When he got up to fetch his things, Zara silently congratulated herself. She also took the opportunity to drink without choking, and it was only after he'd returned and stretched his long body out on top of his carefully positioned sleeping bag that she questioned what she'd just done.

Nothing, she answered herself. *Nothing is going to happen.*

That's what her brain said while her breathing grew shallow and her heart rate blew up and her glands pumped a steady stream of I-want-stuff-to-happen hormones into her blood.

From the corner of her eye she could just make out his figure in the low light. On his back, hands resting on his abdomen, bare feet crossed at the ankle. A couple of feet separated them, yet she could feel his proximity in every cell of her body.

She could not just lie there, saying nothing, doing

nothing. She wanted to talk about something light and easy and safe. Her gaze fastened on the ghostly silhouette of her bike. Their only means of transport in the morning.

"I bet I know why you can't sleep," she said.

He didn't answer.

"I can hear you thinking."

"That's my stomach rumbling," he said.

Zara smiled. "No, it's definitely your brain. You're worried about tomorrow."

That got his attention. She felt the shift of interest, heard the subtle friction as his head turned on his pillow. "What am I worried about, exactly?" he asked slowly.

"About putting yourself in my hands. When you get on the back of my bike."

She'd expected him to scoff at that. Or to suggest that he'd be in charge and she would ride pillion. She didn't imagine Alex Carlisle rode in life's passenger seat too often.

She sure didn't expect the long, still stretch of a pause or his quietly spoken answer. "I'm not worried about putting myself in your hands, Zara."

That answer seemed laced with everything she felt. Every wired strain in her body, every thud of her heartbeat, every shiver of heat in her blood. Man, but she ached to turn on her side, to look into his eyes, to see if they reflected the sensual ache low in her body.

But she didn't, she couldn't, in case she did something silly like inviting him into her hands. He wasn't hers to touch, he wasn't hers to hold.

"What's the first thing you're going to do?" she asked instead. "When we get back to town? I'm thinking about a long, hot shower."

"I'm thinking about eating."

She smiled at that, at the tone, at the certainty, at the dryness. At the fact that she'd inadvertently hit upon the one thing that would take her mind off her other hunger. "Well, yes, but I figure we'll do that at the first roadhouse or café we come across. I'm thinking about one of those big truckie's breakfasts. Bacon and eggs and sausages."

"With mushrooms?"

Her tummy growled and she did too, in sympathy. "Oh, yeah."

"Tomatoes?"

"Grilled and drizzled with cheese."

"Coffee," he said, low and sybaritic. "I don't even care if it's instant."

She made a low *mmm* of assent as she pondered her cup of hot tea. "Afterwards," she continued dreamily a few seconds later, "I'm going to have one of those chocolate bars I foolishly denied myself yesterday."

"For breakfast?"

Frowning, she turned to look at him. "I thought you loved chocolate."

"Never before noon."

"Are you always so disciplined?"

For a moment he continued to stare up at the ceiling, then slowly he rolled his head on the pillow and she felt the burn of his gaze as it fixed on hers. "We'll see."

The breath caught in her throat, a hitch of sound they both heard and understood. A hitch of the knowledge that, despite her earlier avowal of trust, only her sleeping bag and his discipline separated them on this bed.

We'll see.

Those words beat through her with the same constant driving rhythm as the rain on the roof, with the same beat as forbidden desire, strong and thick and unrelenting. "I guess you'll be going back to Sydney," she said. "Once we get out of here."

"If I can't find Susannah. Yes."

"You'll go looking for her? Do you still think you can change her mind?" she asked on a rising note, alarmed at the prospect that nothing had changed.

"Yes, I'll look for her. We need to talk. But I can't make her marry me, Zara."

No, but if he looked at her with that intensity, if he spoke to her in that low, smoky voice… "I'm sure you can be very persuasive."

"When I want to be," he said, and that confidence shivered through Zara in a contradiction of desire and disquiet.

Yet she couldn't leave it alone. Despite the moody heat that licked between them, she was enjoying this soft-voiced exchange in the near dark. "Do you want to be married?" she asked after a second. "I mean you, yourself, not because of the will or your family."

"Yes. I want a family, a wife, a marriage."

"You're…how old?"

"Thirty-five."

"And you waited this long to decide you want to marry? Forgive my bluntness, but I imagine you've not been starved of opportunity."

This time he didn't answer straight away, and she sensed a different tension in his hesitation. "I almost married once before."

Zara felt an odd pressure in her chest, a tightness, a lack of breath. "What happened?"

"She married someone else."

Oh, Alex. What could she say? She recalled his closed, hard expression when he'd asked if Susannah had met someone else. The second woman to have changed her mind. How could Suse have done that to him? The day of the wedding, no less.

Yet she knew he wouldn't want her sympathy. Knew that reaching out to touch him would be a bad, dangerous move. Instead she shrugged, as best one can when lying down, and said, "Her loss."

"Yeah," he agreed, and Zara sensed an ease in his tension. Her heart skipped with a kind of gladness because she had picked the right tone, because she had lifted the mood out of murky waters. "I couldn't marry a woman who didn't want me."

She wasn't sure he meant Susannah and she didn't ask. Suddenly she felt less sympathetic toward her friend and much too sympathetic toward this man she'd grossly misread. So many layers, every one more intriguing, every one adding to her fascination.

"I believe I owe you an apology," she said softly. "I misjudged you."

And Lord help her, this time she couldn't help turning and touching. Just her hand on his. A brief touch, a quick kiss of heat in the dark.

He didn't thank her. He didn't say anything for a moment and then he shook his head and she heard the heavy expulsion of his breath. "I want to get an early start in the morning. How about we try to get some sleep."

"I'll try," she said dubiously and closed her eyes.

Amazingly she slept.

Hours later Zara woke and for a long moment lay perfectly still while she made sense of her surroundings. The storm had passed, leaving behind a quiet broken only by the creak of wet timber expanding and the faint drip, drip, drip of water somewhere outside. The darkness was more complete, and she realized the fire had gone out. Not even an ember sparked to break the solid wall of black. Yet she wasn't cold.

Oh, no, she was very, very warm, snuggled as she was against the intense body heat of the man in her bed.

Surreptitiously she stretched a hand toward the edge of the mattress. The distance she needed to stretch confirmed her suspicion. She had backed into the center of the bed. She had spooned into his hips and curved her legs to trace the line of his.

His arm was thrown over hers, trapping her there. So close she swore she could feel the hard line of him against her backside. Despite at least one sleeping bag in between.

Heart thudding hard in her chest, she fought an almighty surge of temptation to press back against him. To unzip the cursed bag. To turn and touch.

No, no, no, she whispered silently in time with the dripping rainwater. *Move your backside forward. Away. A little wriggle forward, one hip and then the other*

"Zara." The hush of her name washed over her, quiet as the night. Dark as temptation. She stopped wriggling but the impact of his voice—the notion that he too lay awake, hard and hot at her back—rolled through her like molten chocolate. Sweet and thick in her veins and her senses.

"Yes?" she managed to breathe.

"Best you don't do that."

Oh, man, did he think she was shimmying up against him on purpose? That was altogether possible seeing as he still lay on his side of the bed.

Mortified at being caught out, at unconsciously seeking his heat and shelter while she slept, at thinking of doing exactly what he suspected, she resumed her effort to twist away. He made a sound low in his throat that might have been a groan of discomfort. Or disapproval. Then the arm impeding her escape tightened, pulling her back against him.

Zara swallowed. Yup, he was definitely aroused. Very much so.

"I thought you didn't want me to know about that," she said.

The hand at her waist twitched, but when he spoke, his voice was coated with dry amusement. "I think you pretty much know every inch by now."

What could she say to that? Certainly not the wicked response that leaped into her mind and pooled low in her body. Nope, she better not make any crack about how she could get more intimately acquainted with those inches.

"What did you mean by 'best you don't do that'?" she asked.

"You were squirming."

"I was trying to move away without waking you. Why did you pull me back?"

"I like the feel of you against me," he said frankly. "If you just lay still like you've been doing for the last couple of hours, we'll do fine."

Zara exhaled slowly. Felt the spread of his fingers on her abdomen, the tiniest shift in pressure. He expected her to lie still? Now she knew that he touched her, now she knew that he wanted her?

"You've been—" she moistened her lips "—lying there…awake…for hours?"

"Yeah. Awake."

Again that lick of dry amusement. Oh, yeah, he recognized her slight pause for what it was. He knew she'd been thinking of him lying awake and hard for hours.

"Go to sleep, Zara," he said quietly.

Go to sleep? Was he for real? Or had she missed something in the translation?

Using her shoulder and elbow for leverage, she managed to push free of his hold and roll onto her back. Then onto her side to face him. "You expect me to just go back to sleep? As if I don't know that you're aroused?"

"That bothers you?"

She blinked, unsure how to respond. Wishing the night weren't so dark so she could see more than an impression of his strong, dark face. "Shouldn't it?"

"I'm not going to use it for anything. No matter how nicely you ask."

To her credit, Zara's mouth didn't fall open. Much. She drew an audible breath and let it go. Replayed that shockingly candid admission in her mind and let its impact settle. She believed him. Even if she made the moves, if she reached out and put her hand on that hot, hard body, he would resist.

Reflexively she curled her fingers tight into the palm that tingled with the suggestion of touch. Deep inside she felt a rush of sensation, not wild and hot like so many times during this long night, but steady and strong.

A knowledge that this was a man she could trust.

"Because of Susannah?"

"Until I talk to her, until I hear it from her lips, we're still engaged."

And then? The words jumped from her mind to her mouth but she bit them off. And then he would be in another city, another state, another lifestyle far removed from hers. Then, no matter how nicely he asked, there would be nothing.

Susannah might keep them apart now, but in the end there was nothing to keep them together. Nothing but a cabin-fever attraction he had the willpower to resist.

She would do well to take a lesson.

Five

Alex went to sleep hard and woke the same way. No surprise there, since he lay wrapped around a woman who'd stirred his juices from the instant he'd clapped eyes on her.

He wasn't sure why he'd insisted on dragging her back into his embrace when she'd woken in the night, except that he did enjoy the feel of her long, strong body matched to his. In his sleep he'd enjoyed the fantasy of unzipping her sleeping bag and running his hands over that amazing body.

The fantasy of starting the day with long, slow morning sex.

With a low groan, he edged away from that fantasy and the torturous pleasure of her derriere nestled against him. He must be turning into a masochist. And a supreme optimist if he imagined himself capable of long and slow anything right now.

Rising on one elbow, he stroked a fall of hair back from

her face, then held his breath when she stirred. She slept on but with a frown puckering the skin between her eyebrows. Tension ticked one of the fingers curled around the top of her sleeping bag and her legs shifted restlessly inside its bulky warmth.

She'd moved in her sleep too, not only snuggling closer to his body heat but shifting uneasily as if her mind never rested. Perhaps it was his presence or the aftermath of what must have been a harrowing day. Or perhaps she was simply reciting her anatomy lessons, like she'd told him she did at the traffic lights.

Smiling at that, he slowly traced the length of her exposed arm with the back of his hand. *Scapula. Humerus. Radius and ulna.* He stopped at her wrist, frowning in concentration as he struggled to remember the name of the next bone. She shifted again, rolling her shoulders slightly as if responding to the light pressure of his touch.

He gave up on the bone thing to watch her face, unobserved, in the thin dawn light. To torture himself with not touching more of her smooth skin, with not kissing the sleep-soft fullness of her lips, with not flicking his tongue against that beauty spot on her cheek.

He wanted all that, and sometime during the night he'd accepted that he could want more. He'd entertained the notion that his first gut instinct may have been wrong. That she might be the right woman, but at the wrong time. But until he'd talked to Susannah, he could not tempt himself with possibilities.

I'm sorry, Alex, but I can't marry you today.

In his head he heard Susannah's voice, heard her emphasis on that last word. Until he found her, until he heard her voice finish that statement with *any day*, he was bound to her and to his marriage proposal.

He rolled from the bed, stood and stretched a dozen tight muscles, and watched Zara come awake. It didn't bother him that she caught him standing there beside the bed, sporting only underpants and a massive morning erection. Apparently it didn't bother her either because she took her time looking.

Alex finished rolling his head and shoulders and smiled down at her. "Good morning."

He liked the hazy distraction in her eyes when they rose to meet his. The husky morning edge to her voice when she returned his greeting. "What time do you want to get going?"

He reached for his trousers and started to pull them on. "What time do you suppose that roadhouse will be open for breakfast?"

Unable to get around the obstruction of the tree and his incapacitated rental car, they detoured via a longer alternate route. Several miles before connecting up with the highway, they came upon a tiny settlement with a café-slash-petrol-station-slash-general-store and a handmade sign advertising Home Cooked Meals. Carmel, the cook-slash-waitress-slash-store-owner, told them she did a good trade in lumber trucks.

She told them quite a bit, actually, in intermittent slices of monologue each time she returned to plunk something else on their table. In return they told her how they'd missed dinner and she promised to fill them right back up again.

She'd been working on that ever since.

Between feeding their hunger and Carmel's voluble presence, they'd barely spoken to each other since sitting down at the worn Formica table. But with the edge now off, Alex watched Zara spoon the last of a generous serving of scrambled eggs onto her plate.

She ate with a refreshing lack of self-consciousness, only pausing, her fork midway between plate and mouth, when she caught him watching her. "Please tell me you're not staring at a big smudge of sauce on my chin."

"No. I'm enjoying your appetite." Alex reached across the table and tapped her wrist. "What are these bones called?"

She stared at him, obviously perplexed.

"I was trying to think of the name this morning. Scapula. Humerus. Radius and ulna. I couldn't remember the wrist bones."

"Carpals," she said, frowning.

Carmel returned to gather and stack the finished plates, to ask if they enjoyed it all, to see if she could get them anything else. Alex leaned back in his chair, enjoying the look of confusion on Zara's face as she tried to work out what the bones thing was about. He decided to let her wonder. He liked the way concentration drew her heavy brows together, giving her an almost fierce look. Like an Amazon warrior queen.

"I wasn't going to ask." Carmel paused, her hands filled with plates, her gaze narrowed on his face. "All the while I cooked your breakfast I've been trying to work out why you look familiar, and I just can't work it out."

Alex gave a casual shrug. "I get that a lot."

"You're not on the television then?"

"Not that I know."

"Huh." She shook her head. "You must look like somebody famous."

"I guess that's it." He eyed his empty cup. "Could I trouble you for another coffee, Carmel?"

"That won't be any trouble at all. How about you, love? More tea?"

"Lovely. Thank you," Zara replied but she continued to study him intently, her frown now about curiosity more than confusion. "Do you get recognized often?"

He tracked Carmel's exit to the kitchen. "She only thought I looked familiar."

"Hardly surprising. Your picture's always in the papers for some reason or other. I recognized you as soon as you stepped out of that car yesterday!"

"You had reason to."

She dismissed that with a wave of one hand, then sat in silence while Carmel filled his coffee and muttered something about his TV face.

"Why didn't you tell her who you were?" she asked when they were alone again. "That would have made her day."

"I suspect my generous tip will do that," he said dryly.

"Well, yes, but a celebrity sighting would have been the cherry on top."

"She wanted a TV star."

"Oh, I think royalty would have done just as nicely."

Royalty? Alex made a disparaging sound and shook his head, but her eyes continued to shine with unfulfilled curiosity.

"Does it bother you, the way the magazines love to label you and your brothers with those Aussie royalty tags?"

"No."

Her *huh* sound could have been acceptance. Or disbelief. "You don't mind being referred to as one of the 'Princes of the Outback'?"

"I don't read that garbage." He reached for the sugar bowl. "That's not what bothers me about media interest."

"What *does* bother you?"

"When someone gets hurt."

For a second he concentrated on stirring sweetness into

his coffee, ignoring the bitter taste of experience that rose to coat his senses. But he could feel her sharpened gaze on his face, could feel her curiosity change from teasing interest to serious attention. "Anyone in particular?" she asked.

"My mother." Across the table he met her eyes, sincere and unwavering, and he realized that for once he didn't mind talking about this. He wanted her to know the truth instead of the half-truths and outright lies that had been printed by the gutter press. "They gave her hell when she lived in Sydney, after our sister died of SIDS. Not a great time to have a dozen lenses trained on your face everywhere you went, but they loved capturing Maura Carlisle looking less than glamorous."

"I'm sure they loved the whole story," she said softly. "A beautiful model married to one of Australia's richest men, suffering the same as any grief-stricken mother."

"Couldn't get enough of it," he confirmed. "In the end Chas moved us all to the outback station where he grew up. Mau's rarely left there since."

"Is that why your father wanted this grandchild?" she asked after a thoughtful length of pause. "Because of what losing her baby girl cost your mother?"

"Cost?" Alex frowned at that choice of word.

"She lost a child, a part of her, a piece of her heart. And she also lost her freedom to live where she chose." Her eyes, astute and serious, held his across the table. "I can't help wondering if your father maybe felt some guilt over that. I mean, if he weren't so high profile, the press wouldn't have cared and your family wouldn't have been uprooted."

"She was famous in her own right."

"Ah, but never so much as when she married 'King' Carlisle," she said with an edge of wryness. "Then she became the next best thing to royalty."

It bothered him, that sarcastic bite in her voice. Bothered him because this was his family. His parents. "Sounds like you read too many tabloids."

"I try to avoid them, actually. I know how bloody they can be."

"Are you speaking from personal experience?"

She gave the merest shrug, not offhand, not casual. Then she lifted her gaze and the expression in her eyes, fierce and dark as if she were fighting to keep emotion at bay, drove the air from his lungs. "Would you believe my mother suffered at their hands once, too, a long time ago?"

"She was famous?"

"She had her fifteen minutes." A smile drifted across her lips, a lopsided smile tinged with irony and with a sadness that squeezed tight in his chest. "Nothing in the Carlisle mold, of course."

He didn't smile back. "Was she an actor or—"

He broke off when Carmel returned for their cups, tidying and wiping and asking if they needed anything else. "Just the bill," Alex told her, his eyes not leaving Zara's face. And when Carmel finally left he leaned forward, intent on finding out what had happened in that fifteen minutes. "Tell me about your mother."

"Oh, that's a long story," she said with another smile.

"It's one I want to hear."

Something shifted in her expression, opened and softened for a singular second. Then she gathered herself and shook her head. "Don't you think we should be going?"

"I'm not in that big a hurry."

"You're not afraid Carmel will suddenly look up in the middle of washing dishes and go, 'I remember now. It's Alex Carlisle. One of those filthy-rich princes!'"

"All right," he said agreeably after a short pause. He saw

her surprise in the slight widening of her eyes and smiled as he got to his feet and walked around to pull out her chair. Then, when she was on her feet, he looked right into those eyes and said, "You can tell me the whole long story another time. When we're alone and won't be interrupted."

Zara told herself it was a throwaway line. He didn't mean that he intended seeing her again, but that didn't prevent the swift grab of longing that shadowed hard on the heels of his words. Not that it mattered. There would be no "another time." No more sharing of confidences or beds.

No more desiring what she could not have.

The ride back to the city, unfortunately, only served to intensify the potent physicality of that desire. Mile after mile, she became more aware of his solid presence at her back, his hands spread over her rib cage, the vibration of the bike between her legs.

Oh, God.

Heat shuddered through her. Heat and memories and the knowledge that only inches separated their bodies. No. She huffed out a quick breath. She did not need to think about the intimacy of his body hard against hers. Or the edge of vulnerability she detected deep in his storm-gray eyes when he talked about his mother's loss.

She needed to picture him looking ridiculously out of place riding pillion in a business suit. She needed to picture him looking out of place on her bike and in her life. In the living room of her tiny Brunswick terrace, for example, among the eclectic mix of furniture slung together from estate sales and secondhand shops.

She needed to picture him sitting on her red leatherette sofa surrounded by her mother's collection of cushions, a rainbow palette of silky fabrics and girlie adornments, while she told him the story of Ginger Love, the stripper. Except she wouldn't because after she dropped him at his hotel, she would never see him again.

Providing Susannah doesn't change her mind.

The possibility fluttered through her consciousness, then lodged tight in her brain and her throat. If Susannah changed her mind and married this man, how could she face them? Her best friend—*her only known family*—and the man she'd fallen in lust with.

Last night he'd told her he couldn't marry someone who didn't want him, but what if Susannah returned ready to wed him and have this baby that mattered so much to his family? How could he refuse?

Sucking in a hard breath, she forced herself to grab hold of the wild black churn of resistance before it spun out of control. She had no business craving Alex Carlisle, even if Susannah didn't want him back.

His home was in Sydney, hers in Melbourne. Their lifestyles were diametrically opposed, their goals in conflict. He needed an immediate family, she needed her degree. She barely kept up with study and the work necessary to pay her bills without thinking about a relationship.

She told herself all this, silently reciting the logic point by point as the miles whizzed by, as the landscape changed from bushland to paddocks to suburbia. Less than twenty-four hours since they'd met, so why did she feel as if she'd known him so much longer? Why did she feel a gathering anxiety as the suburbs turned to cityscape, as they drew closer and closer to their destination?

To the moment when she would say goodbye.

That restless stir of nerves and blood and mind made her drive a little too fast, zipping in and out of traffic and taking side streets to avoid the lights. But no matter how many turns she made, she could not escape the pervasive sense that this last twenty-four hours had changed something key to her happiness.

Oh, the scientist in her scoffed. The cynic sneered and the realist just shook her head and suggested she couldn't afford a speeding ticket.

And when she pulled up outside the elegant facade of the Carlisle Grande Hotel, on the terra-cotta pavement under the gleaming stretch of awning, she still hadn't shaken that unsettling anxiety from her body. It bugged her, the unaccustomed sense of nervous uncertainty, enough that she gave the throttle a half turn, amplifying the high-pitched roar for a few revs, before she turned off the engine.

A liveried doorman started toward them, his face a stern mask of disapproval, but then she saw him double-take. Alex had stepped from the bike and removed the helmet and jacket he'd borrowed from Carmel. The doorman dipped his hat and asked if everything was all right, sir, and various other staff lurked nearby, obviously awaiting instructions.

Alex lurked, too, obviously waiting for her to…what? Because of the broken stand, she couldn't get off the bike but after a couple of seconds she did take off her helmet and shake out her hair. Hard to say goodbye through a Plexiglas visor.

Hard, too, to meet his eyes with her usual directness and to find the words to broach the awkward silence.

"It's been—" *Was there an adjective to describe this last day?* "—interesting. You are not what I imagined, Alex Carlisle."

His gaze slid over her, her bike, the helmet resting on the tank. Back to her eyes. "Likewise, Zara Lovett."

Zara moistened her lips. Her fingers played over her helmet, lifting and releasing the hinged visor, as she struggled over what to say. Goodbye seemed vastly inadequate, yet what else was there?

"I thought you would be ruthless and arrogant and full of yourself."

"What makes you think I'm not?"

For a second she stared back at him, knocked off balance by the impact of that question. Low, quiet, dangerous. "Last night," she told him, recovering. Lifting her chin. "You know you could have had me."

Heat flashed in his eyes. "I know."

Behind them a car pulled up, a distraction, a reminder of where they were and a focus for her thoughts. There wasn't any point extending this. There wasn't anything to say. "Well, you have a fiancée to find and I have study to catch up on. I'd best get moving."

But when she reached for her helmet, he put a hand on her shoulder. She felt the charge right through her leather. "I want to see you again. Is night the best time to call?"

"Don't call," she said quickly. "It's pointless. You're in Sydney and I'm in Melbourne. You want a wife and family. I don't even have time to date. I'm not the woman you want, Alex."

"I'm not asking you to marry me, Zara."

And while she was still dealing with all the conflicting implications of that statement, his hand slid from her shoulder to cup her neck. Then he leaned down and kissed her.

Oh, man. He kissed her, and after the first shocked second of pressure from those unexpectedly cool, amazingly supple lips, she kissed him back.

The response was instant. Her brain shut down. Her complete sensory system quivered with pleasure.

Against the sensitive skin of her nape, his fingers moved

infinitesimally, their touch as soft as the finest silk, the effect a lightning streak of fire in her skin and her veins. Her nostrils flared, drawing in his scent. Not yesterday's cologne but just the musky impression of man.

Not the filthy-rich tycoon, not the ruthless groom, just the man.

Dimly, that registered as significant. Dangerous. And then his tongue stroked her bottom lip and her whole body embraced the glorious idea of danger, heat, *him*. Starbursts of pleasure peppered her senses as she opened her mouth to deepen the kiss, as she silently acknowledged the overpowering sense of rightness that tightened in her chest, then unraveled in a swift silken flow of delight.

Then it was over, gone, a shift of air against her heated face and the blare of a horn from the street. She'd been completely lost in that kiss, and yet she wasn't surprised. Some part of her had known they would be like this together.

His hand slid from her nape to cup her cheek for a moment, and he looked right into her eyes.

"I do want you, Zara. Make no mistake about that."

"We can't always have what we want," she said softly and a muscle ticked in his cheek.

"I know that." He straightened, and as his hand slipped from her face, she felt an intense sense of loss. It wasn't only the breaking of that physical bond, but the sudden grimness she saw in his eyes.

Then he turned and was striding away before she could say the one word she'd been so intent on saying.

Goodbye.

Six

Not having his hands on something he wanted didn't usually perturb Alex. If he wanted that something badly enough, he devised a plan and went after it. In the case of wanting Zara Lovett, however, his hands were tied.

By lunchtime Monday he'd determined that no one knew Susannah's whereabouts and short of implementing a search—he put an investigator on standby, in case she didn't turn up soon—he could do nothing but wait.

And that inactivity, that lack of action, perturbed the hell out of him.

So did the tick of the clock counting down on the deadline for conceiving a baby.

During the long, dark stretch of Monday night, while he stared at the shadows on his bedroom ceiling with the taste and texture and heat of Zara's mouth alive in his senses, he could hear the time passing in endless pulsing beats of his blood. The frustration of knowing he might fail kept him awake. The conflict over what he wanted—Zara—and what he needed—a wife—brought him close to howling.

If Susannah returned wanting to be that wife, what then?

He could go ahead, marry her, and still not make a baby within the tight time frame. And if he did succeed on that front, would it really count as success if no one was happy?

His mother had made her feelings clear when he'd called with the news of his non-wedding. "I watched you together, darling, the night you brought Susannah to Kameruka. I'm so glad she was sensible enough to see what you're too stubborn to admit."

Not stubborn, Alex contended. Just focused on what had to be done. His duty, his responsibility, his contribution to the family that meant everything to him.

Even if that makes no one happy?

Tuesday morning dawned without any answers, and Alex took his simmering frustration to the racetrack to watch his favorite horse gallop. When he saw his brother strolling toward him in the pale, early morning light, he swore softly. He'd learned to deal with Rafe's smart-aleck observations over the years. He no longer let them get under his skin and wind his temper as they'd done in his youth.

Not after his mother had sat Alex down and told him about his biological father, about the tearaway temper that had destroyed his career, his reputation, his every relationship. Alex didn't want any part of the man who'd abandoned his mother. He couldn't do a damn thing about his coloring or the set of his eyes or the distinctive mouth he'd inherited, but he could control his wildness.

And, with Charles Carlisle's steady influence, he had controlled it and mastered it. Most days now Alex didn't even have to try. Today, if Rafe was true to form, it might take some effort.

"Morning, bro." Rafe thumped him on the back in greeting. "Has Irish galloped yet?"

"About to go. Your timing's inspired."

"It is, isn't it?" Rafe often made it to early morning track work, but grumbling and yawning and complaining about the godforsaken hour. This morning he practically hummed with bonhomie.

"Why are you in such a good mood?" Alex asked, lifting his binoculars toward the far side of the track and remembering his brother's distraction the previous week over his brand new wife. "I thought you were having marital problems."

"We were." Rafe sounded happy *and* smug. "But we spent the weekend making up."

"Congratulations."

"You too. Although I gotta say I didn't expect to see you this morning. Shouldn't you be honeymooning?"

Although he gripped his binoculars tighter, Alex managed to keep his voice even, his tone conversational. "It appears you haven't heard my news. The wedding didn't go ahead."

"No shit."

"None," Alex confirmed dryly, binoculars trained on the group of horses milling on the far side of the racetrack and the trainer giving instructions to the jockeys. "She's about to send them off."

Side by side they watched a trio of thoroughbreds set off on their training run, tracking their progress through the whispery threads of mist that curled up from the thick, damp turf.

"Glad to hear you came to your senses," Rafe said after several seconds.

"I didn't. Susannah did."

He felt Rafe's focus shift from the horses to his face. Steeled himself for a smart-aleck observation that didn't come. Instead, when he spoke, his brother sounded serious, if slightly suspicious. "You want to tell me how that happened?"

Alex told him, in a bare-bones fashion that skimmed over the night in the cabin and ended with his current situation in limbo-land. And despite his best intentions, frustration coated every word. "Until I hear from her, I don't know where I'm at."

"I think her not turning up on Saturday is a clear enough message of where you're at, bro."

Irritation crackled in Alex's blood. "'I can't marry you *today*' is not definitive."

"Are you saying you'll marry her if she turns up tomorrow?" Rafe's voice rose, incredulous. "After she left you cold at the altar?"

The horses thundered past their vantage point at a full-stretch gallop. Exasperation and a sense of hopeless futility pounded through Alex with the same thick drumbeat. The binoculars came down. Slowly he turned his head to stare at his brother. "Maybe I don't have any choice."

"Because you like being a martyr? Or because you won't allow Tomas or me our part in this?"

A muscle ticked hard in Alex's jaw. He felt it and took it as a warning to cool down, to take a second before answering. "I gather you're doing your bit."

"As was Tomas, before Angie walked. She could be pregnant now. Catriona, too." Rafe's voice softened on his wife's name. His expression, too, as if that possibility enthralled him. As if his new wife enthralled him.

"You love her, don't you?"

"Like crazy."

Alex shook his head slowly as he watched another bunch of racehorses flash by. Rafe Carlisle, confirmed playboy, struck by Cupid's arrow. Amazing. "I never thought I'd see the day."

"The rest were for fun. I knew Catriona was serious stuff the second I clapped eyes on her."

"Weren't you concussed?"

Rafe shrugged negligently but his gaze remained steady. "Unconscious I'd have still known she was the right woman."

The space following his pronouncement echoed with the retreating beat of galloping hooves for a good thirty seconds. Alex's head echoed with the beat of his brother's words. "What if this right woman—your Catriona—hadn't wanted to marry you? What if she wasn't ready for having babies?"

The creases around Rafe's eyes deepened, his gaze narrowed astutely. "If she's the right woman," he said slowly, "then the baby part isn't going to matter…especially if, for example, my brothers had that covered already. In that case, I'd say 'thank you, bro,' and I'd set about convincing her that I was the right man."

Alex didn't thank his brother for that advice before he left the track. He didn't thank him later that night, either, when Rafe called to let him know that Tomas and Angie were back together and setting a wedding date. Rafe used the occasion to casually ask, "Who is she?" to which Alex deadpanned, "I have no idea who you're talking about."

He had no intention of saying anything or doing anything until after he'd talked to Susannah. He didn't know if he could take Rafe's advice, if he could dispense with his familial responsibility, if it turned out he had a choice.

On Thursday, Susannah called.

She told him she couldn't marry him and relief flooded through Alex like a dam gate had opened. Later, he knew, that sense of reprieve would get spliced with guilt and the sense that he was letting down the man who had given him so much, who had made him everything that he was and everything that he wasn't. But for now, he could think no further than the moment, could feel no more than delight and satisfaction because now nothing stood between him and Zara.

That night he picked up the phone and then put it down again. He didn't call her on Friday either because he knew a phone call wouldn't be enough. He flew down to Melbourne instead.

Before his jet landed in the southern capital late on Friday afternoon, Alex knew exactly where to find Zara. Inside *this* fitness club. Satisfaction and anticipation jostled for supremacy in his gut as he flashed a smile at the receptionist.

The smile—and the fact that her eyes widened in recognition—helped when he asked if he could take a look at the facilities. Of course, then he had to stave off her enthusiastic offer to act as tour guide.

"Not necessary," he told her briskly. "I'm only interested in seeing your weights room."

"To your left and you'll see the sign, but it's no bother, Mr. Carlisle, really…."

Alex was already moving, and with every long stride his expectancy sharpened. For the last twenty-four hours he'd kept that keenness under tight restraint, but as he pushed through the door the rhythmic clank of weights swelled in the air and through his senses. So did his anticipation. His eagerness to meet Zara on equal terms, man and woman, without the will or Susannah strong-arming them apart.

He sensed she would have used this week to shore her I-don't-have-time-for-dating defenses. That's why he hadn't rung, why he'd chosen to surprise her and put her off balance again.

His eyes zeroed in on her instantly…or on her reflected image in the long mirrored wall. For a moment he stood riveted to the spot, drinking in the sight of that killer body at work.

She wore a similar outfit to last weekend. One of those racing-back athletic tops that bared shoulders and arms and the flat stretch of her midriff. Matching shorts—today's color was sunshine yellow—with a pair of stripes tracing the flow of her hips and outer thighs.

He watched the stripes bend and flex as she demonstrated a deep squat, then uncurl in a long, easy flow of limbs. The need to touch, to trace that path with the slow glide of his palms, crackled hot in his blood. When she switched modes, from demonstrator to hands-on instructor, Alex noticed she wasn't alone.

He'd known, of course. That's why she was here. It's what she did as a personal trainer.

He knew all this, yet when she put her hands on the man—when Alex saw the sandwiching touch, one hand on his abs, the other his lower back—an acid burn of jealousy seared his gut. Perhaps she actually heard the steam of that reaction, because suddenly she stilled. Her spine stiffened, her shoulder blades snapped back, and their gazes collided in the mirror. Her eyes widened, sparking with shock and something else.

Oh, yeah. It was still there. The same bolt of attraction. The same smoldering charge of awareness.

She said something to her client, bent to pick up a towel, then started to cross the room toward him. Her eyes flicked over his suit, rested a tick on his mouth. Remembering the heat of their kiss? Recalling his taste in her blood?

Heat burned in Alex's veins. He wondered what the half dozen or so members working on the resistance machines would think if he greeted her like he ached to. If he put his hands on her shoulders and rolled her around against the wall and kissed her until neither of them could remember where they were or why they hadn't kept on kissing last Sunday.

She stopped in front of him. Alex managed to keep his hands at his sides but he couldn't manage another smile. "Hello, Zara."

"Alex." With her usual steady confidence, she met his eyes but a note of wariness crept into her voice. "Why are you here?"

"To see you," he said simply.

Expression guarded, she stared back at him. "Why didn't you call first?"

"Would you have agreed to see me?"

Her lips tightened and her gaze rolled away. Perhaps he should have skipped the awkward introduction and explanation and gone with the kiss.

"So, you found out where I was working? How did you do that?"

"I called Personal Best. Jen was very helpful."

Her brows pulled together in vexation. "She shouldn't have told you I was here. That's not—"

"Don't blame Jen. I told her you would want to see me. I said we were…friends."

The way he lingered over that last word, investing it with an extra layer of meaning, brought her gaze rocketing back to his. "And she believed you? She actually believed I was 'friends' with Alex Carlisle?"

"Apparently," he said mildly. "Or she wouldn't have told me where to find you. Would she?"

No. The answer sparked in her eyes a second before she exhaled an audible breath. Before she lifted her towel to wipe the sheen of perspiration from her face. "Well, I can't talk now. Even to 'friends.' I'm working. I have a client."

"I noticed," he said evenly, taking the towel from her hands. Dabbing at her throat. "You missed a bit."

Under his hand, he felt her reflexive swallow and paused with the towel against her skin. His eyes lifted to hers in time to see the spark of response. It caught alight in his body.

"Are you always so hands-on?" he asked, slowly wiping across her collarbone, dipping into the hollow above. "With your clients?"

"Robert wasn't using his core muscles. I was instructing. Doing my job."

Of course she was. He had no right to this primitive possessive burn. None.

He slung the towel over her shoulder and met her eyes again. "Have dinner with me."

"I can't. I—"

"Don't make excuses. Jen told me this was your last client. You have to eat, I have to eat. I would enjoy your company."

She started to shake her head.

"Come on," he coaxed. "You know you want to."

For some reason that made her take a step back. Not physically, but mentally. He saw the grab of focus in her eyes and could feel the rejection coming off her in waves.

He'd expected this response, had planned for it, but that didn't make it any easier to take.

"It's just a meal, Zara. And while we eat I can tell you about Susannah."

Her eyes widened. "She's back? You've seen her? When? Where was she? Why hasn't she called me?"

"She isn't back. She's on her way to America. Come to dinner and I'll tell you the whole story."

Zara agreed to meet him at the restaurant because, a) she had to know what was going on with Susannah, and, b) if she wanted to keep this "just a meal" then she wasn't inviting him anywhere near her home, and, c) same with his hotel, only more so.

But when she stepped off the tram and saw him on the opposite side of the road, waiting outside Caruso's and scanning the street with the kind of restless impatience she recognized in her own blood, she knew she'd been fooling herself about why she'd agreed to meet him.

She'd been fooling herself, too, in thinking her choice of restaurant—a friendly, boisterous, Italian place—might make him feel uncomfortable and out of place. Ha. He'd dispensed with the corporate suit but still looked like a million dollars in dark trousers and a blue-gray shirt.

The same as in the gym two hours earlier, she couldn't stop staring at the hard, chiseled beauty of his face. Couldn't stop the memories of his kiss from unraveling in silky ribbons of response, a long yearning streamer of desire for *this* man, no matter how wrong, no matter how inopportune, no matter how destructive.

You shouldn't have agreed to see him, Zara. You know that. Turn and walk—no, run!—away before it's too late.

Except her feet remained rooted to the spot, not going

forward but not doing the smart thing and running away. And he saw her then, his restless gaze finding her face through the traffic and not veering for several long, breathless moments. *Run now,* her brain screamed, as he started toward her, his progress stalled by the rattling passage of two trams, one after another.

By the time he'd dodged both trams and several cars to reach her side of the road, by the time he'd paused to take in her batik skirt and vintage silk shirt and loose flow of hair, it was much too late to run. Then he smiled and took her hands and drew her so close she could feel the heat emanating from his body and her knees went weak with longing.

She swore he sniffed at her throat, just below her ear, before he kissed her cheek and drew back, still holding both her hands.

"What?" she asked, mesmerized by the hot pall of appreciation in his eyes and the kick of his smile.

"Just seeing if you smell as good as you look."

Oh, yeah, it was much too late.

She was an absolute goner.

Seven

After they ordered, Zara asked about Susannah and Alex told her about the phone call.

"Apparently there's another man," he said in an even voice.

Zara's heart turned over. *Oh, Alex. Why would she want another man when she had you?* "Who is he? When did she meet him? How?"

"Someone from her past, apparently, who turned up again out of the blue. An American, obviously."

Bowled over by this turn of events, by not knowing about any major man in Susannah's past, Zara slumped back in her chair. She mulled over the signs from last week, when Suse had seemed distant and distracted. Then she considered the even, impassive way in which Alex had imparted the news. "Are you okay with this?"

"It would be hypocritical of me not to be," he said wryly. "Given last weekend."

Given meeting her. Given that kiss. Given the way he was looking at her now.

"Nothing has changed since last weekend," she told him, wishing she could make her body believe the words. "I don't want you to read anything into me being here."

"This is just a meal." He lifted one shoulder and both corners of his mouth, ever so attractively. "That's all."

Except dinner with Alex Carlisle was so much more than "just a meal." One moment she talked and laughed in complete relaxation, the next she was struck dumb by the rush of heat when their legs brushed under the table and their eyes caught and captured the flame.

But there was more than the sexual thrall, more than the mesmerizing swirl of storm-blue eyes and her fascination with the lines that bracketed his face when he smiled, in the dusting of dark hair on the back of his hands and forearms. There was the sultry beat of desire when she thought about those hands on her body, and the ache of restraint because hers weren't on him.

But mostly there was captivation, in his company and his conversation, in the connection she felt as they shared slivers of their lives, and in his attentiveness. Having a man like Alex Carlisle hanging on her every word was a heady, rich, empowering sensation that transcended anything she'd ever felt.

If she weren't so enthralled and, yeah, turned on, she knew that would bother her on numerous levels. She shouldn't need a man's approval and attention to feel *this* good, *this* alive, *this* female. But she did feel all those things and for once she shoved all the be-responsible, think-about-tomorrow, look-after-your-own-happiness stuff aside, and immersed herself in the moment.

When he finally asked about her mother—as he'd promised after breakfast five days before—she only smiled and met his eyes over the rim of her coffee cup. "I wondered when you'd get to that."

"I wondered if you'd volunteer the information."

"What do you want to know?"

"Everything."

And despite the casual exchange of lines, despite the smile on her lips and her relaxed posture, Zara felt a shiver of trepidation deep inside. This represented a new level of dinner conversation. This was the most important part of her life. This was everything that had shaped her world.

One part of her wanted to share, but another part warned her about the promise she'd made to Susannah and how easily that could be exposed if she didn't tread warily. "You want to know why Mum was in the papers?" she asked, knowing she couldn't avoid sharing this part. Hating what this would expose, nonetheless.

"That's a start."

Zara nodded. Drew a breath. And decided she might as well tell it like it was. In straight, bald terms. "One of the tabloids found out she was mistress to a powerful man. He was a big name in business and society and he'd set her up a flash house, bought her all the pretty things."

"Doesn't sound like much of a story," he said mildly, meeting her eyes across the table.

"Possibly not. Except Mum was pregnant. At the same time as his wife, as it happens. Big story, big scandal, big scarlet woman."

"She didn't know he was married?"

"She didn't know Mi—" She caught herself before the name slipped out. "His wife was pregnant, that's for sure. She didn't talk about him much, but I rather think he'd spun her the usual lines. His marriage was over but he couldn't end it for business reasons. To protect his fortune and his status, I imagine. Then, when this story broke, she found out he'd been less than truthful."

He didn't say anything for a long moment and Zara resisted a fierce urge to fill the silence by defending her mother for the unforgivable. To justify something Zara had only started to comprehend in the last week, since she'd met this man. Because, even knowing Alex Carlisle belonged to another woman, she had been tempted.

You know you could have had me.

I know.

"This was your father?" he asked, breaking into her thoughts.

"Yes, but please don't ask about him. Nothing personal. I don't talk about him to anyone." She attempted a smile and felt the tug of its tight, bitter edges. "It's not good for my sanity."

"What about your mother's?"

"Oh, she got over him. She had her pride and she was always practical. She had a baby to raise."

"Appears she did a fine job."

"Yes. She did," Zara said with no false modesty. "No one had a better mother than I did."

Something flitted across his expression as he watched her, an element she'd not seen before. Intense but with softer edges, it stole her breath and sounded alarm bells in her head. A warning that this man could steal so much more than her breath, that he could make her want too much and leave her wanting more.

Then his eyes narrowed a smidgen, deepening the creases at their edges.

"What's that look about?" she asked suspiciously.

"I'm just picturing you as a little girl." His lips lifted into a smile and as quickly as that he turned the mood around. "Did you play at being a doctor?"

"Yes." Relief washed through her as she smiled back at him. Relief that he'd not wanted to pursue that serious moment, or press her about the father she didn't want to know. That instead he'd chosen to lighten the tone. "I loved my red plastic stethoscope and the medical encyclopedia best."

"Interesting choice of reading."

"Oh, my mum read me traditional stories, too."

His lips quirked again. "Fairy tales?"

"You betcha. She wanted me to know that Little Red Riding Hood and her girlfriends made some singularly bad decisions regarding big, bad wolves and kissing frogs and the like. She brought me up to believe I could rescue myself rather than waiting around for a stray prince or woodcutter."

"Cynical," he said, eyes narrowed, thoughtful, "but interesting."

"Realistic," she corrected, "but why interesting?"

"At the cabin last weekend you said you would only marry for love."

"Yes, and one day I will. In the meantime I'm not hanging around waiting for my prince."

Unfortunate wording, she realized, when his eyes darkened with the impact of her word choice, but she refused to acknowledge that link to him. He wasn't her prince. He wasn't a prince at all, to anyone but the trash media she despised.

Lifting her chin a fraction, she met his eyes. "In the meantime I'm doing what I've always wanted to do."

"You've always wanted to study medicine?"

"Pretty much. I danced when I was little, and then I got into sports. Along the way I developed a fascination for the human body and how it works, so that was always my first choice for university. I'd only done one year when Mum got sick."

"You deferred your course to look after her?"

"Yes." She shifted in her seat, uneasy talking about that soul-destroying time as her mother's damaged nervous system gave out and her muscles wasted away. "Afterwards it took a while to get myself together. When I did resume my course work I was even more determined to get my degree."

"Because you promised her."

"There is that, but also…I wanted to do something that would make a difference. It's hard to explain but it's like…it's like I didn't want her suffering to have been in vain." She finished up in a rush and then rolled her eyes self-consciously. "I know that sounds ridiculous."

"No. It doesn't."

The quiet certainty of his voice, in his expression, made her heart trip in her chest. She drew a deep breath, cautioned herself again about feeling too much, responding too much. Falling too hard.

"What about your father?" he asked after a moment. "Would he be proud of you too?"

The automatic response, the I-don't-give-a-damn-what-the-bastard-thinks, froze under his serious regard. For some reason she felt a connection, an emotional accord, and another answer altogether slid easily from her tongue. "I always thought I didn't care, but before he died you know what I discovered? There was this rogue part of me that wanted to make a mark. To be a somebody, a success, so that one day he might come looking for me. That he might want to know me."

"You went looking for him?" he asked slowly. Astutely.

"When I couldn't look after Mum anymore, when she

moved into care, I had to sell the house. Anyway, I found those paper clippings. She'd kept them all, I don't know why, so he wasn't difficult to find."

"And you wished you hadn't bothered?"

"No. Actually, I'm glad I found him." Frowning, she searched for the words to explain what sounded like a paradox. "I guess I'd always wondered if things had been different—if he hadn't been married or if he'd divorced his wife—what might have been. Meeting him cemented that we were better off on our own."

"You didn't hit it off, huh?"

"Nicely put." And for once she realized that talking about Edward Horton hadn't twisted her insides into knots. No aftertaste soured her mouth. An ironic smile curved her lips as she considered another aspect of those dark months. "On the positive side, I was into kickboxing at the time and meeting him had a big impact on my aggression."

Smiling at that, he reached across the table and trapped her hand in his. And when she looked into his eyes Zara actually felt something inside her give. "We had that in common," he admitted softly.

"You kickbox?"

A joke, sort of, but he didn't laugh. "The aggressive streak because of a father who didn't want to know me. Except I got lucky when my mother married Chas. I didn't need to go looking. There was nothing I wanted from my biological father, I had nothing to say to him."

"Is that why honoring your stepfather's will matters so much?"

"It seemed the least I could do."

"And now?" she asked.

"My brothers tell me there's still hope. Tomas and Angie

are back together. Rafe and his wife have worked out their problems, apparently."

"That must be a relief."

"Of sorts." His shrug looked tight, not quite casual. "I don't like that I can't uphold my end of the pact."

No, he wouldn't. Zara could see that in the stormy swirl of his eyes and the tight set of his mouth. He would view it as failure. "Worse," she said solemnly, "to have married for the sake of the pact and then regretted it afterward."

"Do you regret coming here tonight?" he asked after a moment.

"No."

Heat sparked in his eyes as he turned her hand over and linked their fingers. Heat and everything else that had passed between them during what had never been "just a meal." And in that instant she was back on the street, her gaze trapped by the smoky intensity of his, thinking *I am a goner.*

"What are we going to do," he said, low and gruff, "about this?"

The background noise faded to a dull blur as all Zara's focus centered on him. The unsmiling intensity of his expression, the silent appeal in his eyes, the heated charge of his touch. "I don't know."

"Would you like to come back to my hotel room?"

Her simple "yes" almost brought Alex to his knees. So unexpected, so honest, so exactly how this night had to end. He didn't question her motivation. He paid the bill; he ushered her outside; he made small talk about the food and the balmy spring night while they waited to hail a taxi in busy Sydney Road.

On the surface he maintained his cool. Inside anticipation

honed his focus to a keen knife's edge. He had to get this woman—this woman he wanted more than his next breath—back to his hotel and into his bed before she reconsidered.

A cab pulled up on the opposite side of the street and he took her hand, towing her through the traffic until he could steer her into the back seat. He didn't see any reason to let go of her hand. He liked the strength of her grip, the intimacy of their linked fingers, the charge of heat when he rested their joined hands on his thigh.

The grip of tension when her fingertips brushed the fabric of his trousers.

That touch, innocent but incendiary, blew whatever he'd been discussing with the cabbie clean out of his brain. Finals football? The pre-election polls? The upcoming spring racing carnival? Frowning, he struggled out of the lust fugue and forced himself to focus on the driver's laconic commentary because, hell, if he started thinking about those fingertips on his skin, if he gave in to the urge and lifted her hand to his lips, if he tasted a hint of her sweet scent then he would be lost.

"Got a runner in the Cup this year?" the cabbie asked.

Alex knew he'd been identified before this giveaway question. The driver's eyes kept darting to his mirror, watching, not missing a thing. Hence his caution with Zara. He'd kicked himself to kingdom come and back again after last week's recklessly public kiss outside the hotel. It's a wonder *that* hadn't appeared front page in the tabloids!

Tonight he was being more circumspect. Hand-holding was fine. Anything involving tongues was definitely behind closed doors.

"Irish Kisses is entered," he supplied in answer to the cabbie's question about the Melbourne Cup. "We'll see how her form holds up in the meantime."

"Guess a lot can happen in…how long till the big one?"

Alex did the calculation. "Five weeks next Tuesday."

And, yes, a lot could happen in that length of time. His horse could go lame, get sick, train off—any one of a dozen variables could rob him of a starter in Australia's richest horse race.

Yet tonight all he could think about was whether or not, in five weeks' time, he'd still be holding Zara Lovett's hand. If she would be at his side in the stands cheering Irish home. If she would celebrate with him, or console him afterward with her silky sweet-tasting kisses.

Reflexively his grip on her hand tightened. Her fingers curled hard against his thigh and that touch arrowed straight to his groin. Heat washed through his skin, so intense he felt perspiration break out down his spine.

"I'm not going anywhere," she said softly, squeezing his hand. Subtly reminding him to ease off the pressure. He did, stroking his thumb across her knuckles, rolling the tension from his shoulders, breathing a silent sigh of relief when the taxi pulled in to the hotel driveway.

Finally—and only because he had to—he released her hand so he could pay the fare.

And when he closed the door and straightened, he realized they were standing in the exact spot where he'd first tasted the lush temptation of her mouth on Sunday. Their gazes met and everything he'd felt in that moment, everything that clamored through him now, was reflected in her whiskey eyes. All he could think about was kissing her again, same place, same way, except this time they would walk away together. All the way to his bed.

Circumspection be damned, he closed the car's-width space between them, cupped her face in one hand and gave in to his fierce need.

One kiss, tempered with a world of restraint, while the stroke of his thumb along her jaw and the burn of passion in his eyes told her that this was only the start. Never dropping his gaze, she stretched closer so her body brushed his in a dozen fleeting places and the subtle flick of her tongue drove a groan from his lust-tight throat.

"Inside," he growled at her ear. "Before we draw a crowd."

She laughed, low and husky and erotic.

Oh, yeah. He would definitely have to find a way to make her laugh once they got naked. Her laughter, her hands, her legs, the silky shimmer of her shirt as she turned into the glare of the lobby light—she blew him away on so many levels, had done so too many times to count these past hours.

This woman, his gut told him as he took her hand and led her through the lobby, *is the one you've been waiting for.*

The clarity of that knowledge didn't shake him. Last weekend he'd known, at the same instinctive level, that more than physical attraction forged this connection. But he'd walked away because of the will and what he took as his duty.

"Hey." Tugging on his hand, she drew him out of his reverie. "Whatever you're thinking about—stop!"

"What if I'm thinking about you?"

"I hope you weren't, actually."

Alex pulled up short and turned her toward him. "You don't want me thinking about you?"

"Not if it makes you look so…intense."

"Ah, but you do make me feel intense," he said, tightening his grip on her fingers. "Whenever I think you might change your mind about stepping into this elevator."

Their gazes tangled and the moment hung with renewed tension, with the hint of wariness that stole across her face.

Alex's heart kicked with sudden fear but he kept his gaze direct. Unflinching. A part of him warned against pushing too hard and scaring her off, but at this moment he simply could not do light and easy. Until he had her upstairs, a smile was impossible. "Make up your mind, Zara. Here and now."

"My mind is made up," she said after the briefest pause. "If I don't do this, I will only spend another week wondering."

"Wondering?"

One corner of her mouth lifted in the smallest hint of a smile. "About whether this will be as good as I've imagined."

Relief poured through Alex as he pulled her closer, relief and a parallel stream of desire because she'd been imagining this—imagining him in her bed—all week. He threaded her hair behind her ear, stroked his fingers down its silken length and saw the spark of response in her eyes.

"Don't worry, sweetheart." He pressed a brief, hard kiss to her lips, then turned them both back toward the elevator. "It'll be better."

Eight

Alone in the elevator, Alex gave in and kissed her like he'd wanted to in the lobby, under the portico, in the taxi. In the street outside the restaurant. In the gym earlier that afternoon. He wound his fingers in her hair and pulled her hard against his body and simply immersed himself in the mind-numbing sweetness of her mouth.

That taste, he knew, was already under his skin, in his blood, hot-wired into his hormones. One sip and they raged into life, screaming for more. He kissed her until the doors opened on the hotel's top floor, and once he had her inside his suite he backed her against the door and kept on kissing her until they were both breathing harder than after their run through the sleet.

Winded, knocked off center by the power of his need, by the fevered roar of blood in his ears, Alex leaned his forehead against hers, flattened his hands against the door and struggled for control. He had, at least, to get her into his bedroom before he tore her clothes off and gave himself up to this raging need.

The hell of it was he didn't want to tear her clothes off. He wanted to undress her slowly so he could savor her amazing body, inch by silky inch. He wanted to seduce her, for Pete's sake, into giving him much more than her body.

"I had hoped to offer you a drink." His voice was a deep mixture of arousal and wryness. "To put on some music. To show you my smooth side."

After a second her hands slid from his neck, down his chest to his sides. "Which *is* your smooth side, Alex? Left or right?"

That surprised a laugh from him, a laugh that snagged in the middle when she stroked a hand up and down one side and then the other. A simple touch made intricate by the extravagance of his body's response. Or perhaps by the way she tipped her head back against the door and studied him through half-lidded eyes, her hair mussed by his hands and her lips full and sultry from his kisses.

"Maybe you need to work that out for yourself," he said, levering himself slowly off the door. Spreading his arms wide, he dared her with both body language and his steady gaze to find her own answer.

Heat flared golden in the depths of her eyes and resounded low in Alex's body. A challenge given. A challenge accepted.

She rolled off the door and Alex smiled at his own unconscious description. Yeah, she rolled…or maybe flowed. Whatever, it was a long, sinuous unraveling that he wanted to freeze-frame in his memory.

Hell, who was he kidding? He loved everything about the way she moved. Sometimes full of energy and purpose.

Sometimes loose and athletic. Sometimes with smooth leonine grace.

Like now, he thought, as she circled him, not touching, just studying him like a hunter on the prowl. A lithe, agile hunting cat, hungry for his body. His every muscle bunched with anticipation, tightened with heated arousal at the thought of her stalking him, taking him down, her mouth on his body.

She disappeared behind him, the flutter of her exotic patterned skirt a whisper of sound and motion, her scent in the air and in his nostrils as he waited. Waited for her touch until he thought he might snap. And then he sensed her closeness, felt the warmth of her breath between his shoulder blades an instant before her hands skimmed down his arms, then repeated the flat-palmed glide up his sides and down his back.

Frustration twitched in his flesh. He wanted more. He wanted those hands beneath his shirt, that breath on his skin. That mouth on his body.

She circled back to the front and their gazes collided. "Hard to tell which is your smooth side." Her voice reflected her eyes. Hot. Aware. Turned on. "You're hard as a rock."

And she hadn't touched him anywhere below the waist.

"You need a closer inspection." He lifted a hand, brushed his thumb across her lips. "Why don't you undress me?"

Her lips quivered under his touch. "Here?"

She had a point. They stood a scant two feet inside the door. A whole spacious suite beckoned. A king-size bed, with the best linen Carlisle money could buy, lay turned down and waiting.

But still…

His thumb ghosted across her cheek, lingered on the

beauty spot. "I'm not fussy about where. You walk into a room and you're all I see. You touch me and everything else fades to black."

Her breath hitched, a sound of wonder, of wanting, and she turned in to his body, so close her skirt skimmed against his thighs and their knees brushed. Warm breath shuddered against his chin, his throat. "I think I just discovered your smooth side."

"It's not a line, Zara. It's the truth."

For a second she went still, and he sensed her weighing that, analyzing it in her sharp brain, and then her fingers lifted to touch his abdomen and chest in a half-dozen places. The merest drift of a caress. The hottest lick of flame.

Alex sucked in air. Her scent, sweet, warm, female, went straight to his head. He trapped her hands against his chest, held them against the thickened drumbeat of his heart, before drawing them to his top button. "Take off my shirt. Please, Zara. I want to feel these hands on my skin."

He felt the flutter of response in her hands, or perhaps it was his flesh that shuddered because when he dropped his hands away she started unthreading buttons with surprising sureness, her fingers quick and steady until they neared his waist. Then she fumbled with delicious effect. Warm breath huffed against bared skin and her knuckles dragged over his tensed abs while she battled with that last button.

Finally, she grabbed two handfuls of shirt and pulled it free of his trousers and the last button gave. Then her hands were on his chest. Her hands and her mouth and the hot murmur of her breath as she said, "I've thought about touching you like this. All night."

"I've been dreaming about it." His hands combed through her hair, let the cool tresses play against his hot skin. "All week."

"Really?"

Oh, yeah. And not just like this. He'd dreamed of those long, elegant fingers, that lush siren's mouth, on him everywhere. "You have no idea."

"Maybe I do."

"Really?" he asked, echoing her question, her tone.

He felt her smile against his skin, felt it seep into his flesh and saturate his blood. "Did you only dream about *me* touching *you?*"

"Is that a hint?"

Her thumb grazed his nipple. "Was I too subtle?"

Alex laughed, low and lazy. He let his hands slide to her shoulders and down her back. Less than a minute ago he'd been too edgy to contemplate lazy or any laughter that wasn't wound as tight as his impatience. But she'd surprised him again with her humor.

Surprised him with how easy she was to be with.

Dipping his thumbs under the hem of her shirt, he stroked the warm skin beneath. His fingers spanned her waist—beneath the silky drape of her shirt—and he started to walk her slowly backward, into the sitting room. "When I was waiting outside the restaurant, wondering if you'd show up—"

"I wouldn't have sent you out there," she cut him off, sharp and affronted, "and then stood you up!"

"Good to know."

"I would have called."

He stopped walking. Ducked down to look into her face. "You thought about doing that, didn't you?"

"At least a dozen times," she admitted. "Every time I tried to call Susannah. Every time I changed my clothes."

"I'm glad you didn't."

"So am I."

The honesty in her words and her steady gaze settled rich and warm in his chest. He had to kiss her again, not with the unrestrained hunger of before but slow and deep and giving. He kissed her mouth and the strong line of her jaw and the little spot on her cheek. "I approve your final choice," he said when he moved on to her ear. "In case you were wondering."

"My final choice?"

Gathering the soft fabric of her shirt in his hands, he slowly pulled it up and off. "Of clothes. You said you changed a dozen times."

"Well, it wasn't quite that many, but close. I'm not used to thinking about what I'm wearing."

"That's okay." Alex fingered the strap of her bra, let it slide down her arm then followed it with his mouth. His hands glided down her back and over her hips. "I'll think about it for you."

"You're offering to act as my wardrobe consultant?" Her amused question ended on a breathy hitch when he gently bit the skin of her shoulder then laved it with his tongue.

"Sure." Slowly, inexorably he bunched up the material of her skirt. "I'll choose your clothes for you as long as I get to take them off."

A smooth line, Alex thought, liking that he had his edginess, the wildness he loathed, back under control. Rewarding himself by drawing up her bunched skirt and letting his knuckles graze the backs of her thighs and the tight curve of her backside…the tight *naked* curve of her backside.

For a fleeting second his fingers fisted in the soft fabric of her skirt. He sucked in a quick breath through his teeth. Then he let that air—plus all the gathered folds of her skirt— go so he could cup those tight naked curves with his palms.

"A G-string," he breathed.

"Is that the underwear you would have chosen, as my wardrobe consultant?"

In answer he drew her hard against his body. Stroked his hands over her warm, smooth skin and absorbed her shudder of response with a long, wet kiss. And when the lust dimmed to a dull roar and his brain cleared enough to distinguish his surroundings again, he resumed walking her toward the bedroom.

Before they made it to the bed, he managed to prize his hands from her body long enough to undo the waistband of her skirt. He took a half step back to watch it slither past her hips, to study those long, toned, runner's legs, to imagine them locked around his hips, holding him deep inside her body. The pulse of sex started to beat through his blood, a hard hum of insistence that filled his senses, and then her hands were on his trousers, an exquisite torture of unbuttoning and unzipping, of touching but not touching nearly enough.

Their eyes met and shared a wordless message of heat and urgency and need. With swift hands and quick catches of breath, they shed the rest of their clothes and sank together to the turned-back bed, rolling in a heated slide of skin against skin, of passion-warmed bodies against the cool expanse of sheets. Again their eyes met and of an accord they slowed, steadied, stilled…until Alex turned them one more rotation and settled on his back.

For the moment he had Zara exactly where he wanted her. Stretched on top of him, her breasts grazed his chest with every breath, her legs tangled with his. She was all sleek curves and finely toned muscles, long and strong and perfect. Slowly he slid his hands over her back, adjusting the weight of her hips until she cradled his arousal between her thighs.

But what froze him in that instant wasn't the fit of their bodies or the teasing lure of her moist heat. It was the intensity of her expression as she looked down at him.

The rush of empowerment, the sense that he'd waited forever to look into this woman's eyes while she took him into her body, stalled the breath in Alex's lungs and squeezed viselike in his chest.

For a second it was too much, a blinding flash of fear that he might give more than he wanted, and then she leaned down and kissed him and drove the beast away with the honeyed taste of her passion. He twisted his hands in her hair and held her there, bound to his mouth and slowly melting over his body, yielding to the thick, insistent heat between his legs.

Longing coiled strong and low in his gut. The desire to spread her wider and push inside. To claim her in the most primitive way, naked and unprotected. His hand traced the length of her spine, and she arched and stretched against the pressure, humming with pleasure into their kiss, against his lips, into his mouth.

Alex's need flexed, stretched, pulsed. He palmed her hips and held her there, hot and wet against him, the worst and the best of tortures. Then with a low growl he rolled her onto her back. "You have no idea how much I want this." All the primitive fire of his need blazed in his eyes and grazed the edges of his voice as he rocked slowly against her. "To forget myself. To forget to ask about protection."

His words seemed to take a second to sink in, but then her eyes widened with understanding, alarm, dismay. Alex felt a jolt of remorse. He shouldn't have admitted to that primitive temptation. Not after last weekend and all they'd talked about. Quickly he rolled away, over to the bedside table and the condoms he'd bought after leaving the gym. *Just a meal* he'd said, while he prepared for much more.

"I can't believe I would forget."

Frowning at the appalled note in her voice, Alex looked back over his shoulder. Her stricken expression caught hard in his chest. "Hey, it's okay."

"No, it's not okay. My mother taught me better. I always carry protection. Always."

He came back to her, pressed a kiss to her mouth, another to the pucker of worry between her brows. "I didn't forget. I'm sorry I sowed that doubt. It was unforgivable. I'll always protect you, sweetheart."

Something flickered in her eyes. Doubt? Skepticism? Whatever, he didn't like it.

"Don't you trust me? If that's—"

"It's not you," she said quickly. Her gaze rested, dark and serious, on his. "Or maybe it is you. You make me forget my common sense." She touched a hand to his mouth and her voice grew husky. "You make me forget…everything."

Her fingers skimmed his lips with silken heat, the sincerity of her words stirred much deeper, richer, hotter. Alex closed his eyes for a second, two, and then he trapped her fingers against his mouth. Opened both eyes and lips as he murmured, "Fade to black."

"You're dangerous," she breathed as he licked across her fingertips. As her quiver of reaction echoed through his body.

"You must have me mixed up with someone else." Eyes never leaving hers, he took her hand from his mouth. "I'm safe." Drew it down his body to touch the part of him he'd made safe. "Steady. Dependable. Reliable."

"Is that how you see yourself?"

"Yes."

For a second she gazed at him speculatively, then her

fingers slid down his shaft and her look turned hot, wicked, erotic. "I'll give you safe." Those teasing fingers wrapped around him and he jerked in response. "But not so steady."

With her hand still on him, Alex's snort of laughter sounded tight and broken. Not steady at all.

"I do believe you're dependable and trustworthy." Her eyes glazed with more than heat, she leaned into him and traced the grooves in his cheeks. With her fingers and then her tongue. "You're hard. And dangerous. And beautiful."

Completely undone by her words, by the sensual whisper of her mouth, Alex struggled to breathe. "That would be you," he managed to say finally. "Beautiful."

"Oh, I'm not beautiful. My sister's beautiful."

"You have a sister?"

"Half." And there was a new tension in her eyes, a dark flash of self-castigation. "Can we not talk about my family?" She cradled him fully in her palm, squeezed gently, insistently. "Can we not talk, at all?"

At the moment Alex couldn't imagine saying anything that wasn't a groan or a plea for mercy. Later, he thought, as he kissed her and palmed her breasts and struggled to contain the swamping wave of desire. Later he would ask questions and inveigle the answers from her sweet mouth. Everything he wanted to know, everything that went on inside her mind, everything that made her strong and vulnerable and completely captivating.

Everything that made her so damn beautiful he ached.

For now he contented himself with learning her body. Everything that made her arch her back and stretch her legs in restless need. Everything that made her hum low in her throat and clutch his head between urgent fingers, holding him to her, enticing him to use tongue and lips more boldly until he lapped up the strong shuddering wave of her first climax.

And when he rose above her, hard and aching with the need to be inside, she met his eyes and slowly drew him into her wet velvet heat. As if she'd divined his need for slow, his craving for self-control, his fervent desire to keep a grasp on the sweat-slippery reins of restraint.

He curbed the incessant need to close his eyes and give himself up to the wild primal instincts of his blood. He needed to be that steady, solid, reliable man he'd created.

"Beautiful," he breathed as she took him to the hilt, and then she squeezed some internal muscles and drove the air hissing from his lungs. Dizzy with lust, with need, with *her,* he struggled to hold himself still, to withdraw inch by inch, to not drive himself all the way in, again and again.

Slowly he pulled back, and she wrapped those amazing legs around him and held him there while she stroked his face and then licked at his mouth. Her taste was on his tongue, in his blood, wrapping him in a thick, sweet cloak. He kissed her throat, nuzzled his face in her shoulder and bit her earlobe as he moved with a slow rocking cadence while the pressure built in the back of his brain and in the tightly bound tension of his muscles.

Her hands slipped through his hair, caressed the long muscles of his back and then gripped his biceps as she arched up to meet a stronger thrust, changing the angle, driving him even deeper and crying out with her pleasure. That was it, that guttural cry of pleasure, that sound of complete abandon, the buck of her hips and the drag of her flesh against his.

"Let yourself go," she murmured, her voice as thick and tight and hot as his body. "Now, Alex, please."

Heat engulfed him. A blazing sensual storm he could no longer fight. He drove faster, harder, deeper until his breath exploded, fast and furious, as his climax came in a blinding explosion of pleasure that swallowed him whole. For a long while he remembered nothing, nothing but the frantic beat of hearts and the cooling sweat of bodies, and running beneath the harsh physical reality like a vein of pure gold lay the innate knowledge that he knew this woman.

That every broken relationship, every woman who hadn't worked out was because he hadn't met this one.

He knew he had to rouse himself, to dispose of the condom. Even through his languor he felt a fierce need to protect her as promised, to protect her during the dangerous afterward. But before he forced his utterly spent muscles into action, he buried his nose in her throat for a second and it came to him, clear and unbidden.

The unnamed element in her scent.

"Almonds."

Zara recalled that one perplexing word muttered against her throat as she stood blinking at herself in his bathroom mirror the next morning. "Almonds," she mouthed silently, shaking her head in bewilderment. What was that all about?

It was an easy something to focus on. One distinct, unthreatening word she'd picked from a thousand that fluttered through her early-morning brain. Not that she was trying to forget or to discount the hours spent in Alex Carlisle's bed. As if she could do either. As if she would ever forget the way he'd loved her, so many times, so many ways.

The hand she lifted to touch a mark on her throat, another on her breast, trembled.

While her pragmatic self came awake knowing what she must do—get dressed, leave while he slept, acknowledge this as a one-night stand—an inner voice murmured that walking away would not be that easy.

Alex Carlisle made love as he did everything—slow,

thorough, intense, with an underlying thread of ruthlessness. As if he couldn't stop until he had bound her to him, body and soul. Her hand dropped from her breast and a shiver of reaction rippled through her over-sensitized skin.

Dangerous. Oh, yes. He was one very dangerous man, making her feel this sated, this different, this beautiful.

Shaking her head at that piece of silliness, she turned away from the mirror. *For heaven's sake, Zara, your nose is still big, your shoulders too wide, your face too long. The mole on your cheek is still a mole no matter how many times he calls it a beauty spot. A masterful mouth and a clever tongue and half a dozen orgasms do not change facts!*

A wry smile curved her lips as she sorted through the items of clothing she'd scooped up from the floor in the near-darkness. Her favorite shirt, her best skirt, her only bra that wasn't a racing-back sports model. And a pair of men's boxer briefs with a designer monogram on the elastic waistband.

Damn.

Quickly she pulled on the rest of the clothing. If she found her underwear on her way out, well and good, but she couldn't spend time searching. She didn't want to wake him. She didn't want to explain. She wanted to get home where she could indulge herself with a long shower, and then she would get dressed in her usual practical, comfortable clothes—with underwear—to face a big day of study.

Right. She inhaled a deep breath, opened the bathroom door, and let out a startled squeak. He stood just outside the door, waiting.

The dark shadow of morning beard, the bed-tousled hair, the broad naked chest made him look not quite civilized. Made her heart thump hard in her chest. So did the look in his eyes as they slowly trailed over her, head to foot.

And the raspy edge to his morning voice as he said, "Good morning. Did you sleep well?"

"Sort of."

He studied her for another second, something dark and primal in his eyes, then he closed the space between them, held her still with a hand cupping her neck and kissed her. Not briefly, not as long as last night's marathon, but very thoroughly. By the time he finished, her heart was racing and the bottom had dropped out of her stomach.

"You're dressed." He rubbed her nape and she curled into that caress like a cat.

Her response resembled a purr.

"Why?"

Frowning, Zara forced herself to straighten and pay attention. "Why…what?"

He curled a finger into the neckline of her shirt and tugged gently. "Why are you dressed?"

"I have to get to work."

"Damn."

And suddenly it was all right, this morning-after intimacy thing. The overwhelming urge to forget work and climb back into his bed was all right, too, since it was an urge he obviously shared. Since it was an urge she couldn't give in to.

She sighed heavily. "Yeah."

"Will you come back?" he asked. "After you finish work?"

How easy it would be to say yes. His hand dipped lower inside her neckline, tracing the slope of her breast, enticing her to accept that easy answer. Her nipples tightened, her heart skittered, but she lifted her eyes and met his gaze steadily. "I have a lot of studying to do. I intend spending the day at the library."

"And after that?"

She moistened her lips. "Alex, I don't think—"

"This wasn't a one-night stand, Zara."

"It was supposed to be just a meal," she countered, not stepping down from the steely resolve in his eyes.

"Let's just see what happens," he said evenly. "I know study is your priority. I know you have your job and not much time."

"No time for a relationship."

Something flickered in his eyes, but before she had a chance to acknowledge the danger, he'd moved closer, cupping her face in his hands, easing her back into the bathroom until she'd backed up against the vanity.

"I'm not going to rush you. I'm not going to impinge on your time." Very, very slowly, he trailed his mouth over her cheek, nuzzling her ear, turning her knees to jelly. He was not playing fair. "Let's just see where this goes? No promises. No commitment. No tomorrow. Just now."

Nine

When Zara exited the library at four o'clock and found him waiting outside, she pulled up so suddenly that a couple of students following behind plowed right into her. She murmured an apology but her eyes didn't shift from his and her feet seemed incapable of resuming motion.

He'd seen her, of course, and as she forced herself to get moving again, as she casually descended the flight of steps to the roadside, he smiled and all those tightly wadded emotions softened to mush. She smiled right back and thought life could only get better if he met her halfway across the wide, pebbled concrete footpath and kissed her.

He didn't. He stood still and straight beside a dark vehicle, and something primitive flitted across his expression. It resounded through her body, heavy in her breasts and tight in her chest and rich in her belly. And beneath the hard hum of that instinctual response, she heard the dull clang of a warning bell.

Caution, Zara. Remember this morning? You only agreed to see him again because he'd promised to take it slow, to make it easy.

Smile tamped by caution, she stopped in front of him. "What are you doing here?"

"Waiting for you."

She gave him a *well, duh* look. "How did you know where to find me?"

"From your housemate."

"Not my boyfriend?" she countered, recalling the first time he'd called her home to finagle information from Tim.

"Not your boyfriend." And there, in his eyes, that same territorial darkness as before.

Zara stiffened her spine, determined to control her female flutter of response. Determined to muster some kind of affront. "You called my home and you asked my housemate about my plans for today?"

"I needed to know what time you'd be finished," he said evenly. "Since you left this morning without saying."

"What if I'd changed my plans? What if I'd told Tim I would be at the library and then I'd left early?"

"Then I'd have missed you and you wouldn't have had the pleasure of my company."

As if that answer weren't enough, he railroaded her with a slow smile and before she could recover, turned and opened the door of his vehicle. A charcoal dark four-wheel drive, probably some luxury model and so up to the minute she could smell the new-car aroma.

He took her backpack, heavy with books, from her arms but Zara stood her ground. "I can't go with you, Alex."

Half-turned toward the vehicle, he paused. His eyes narrowed a fraction. "You said you would see me tonight."

After he'd lifted her onto the cool, wet vanity in the hotel bathroom. After he'd discovered, with devastating effect, that she hadn't found her panties.

That knowledge, that memory burned dark in his narrowed eyes and sparked all kinds of embers in Zara. "You didn't play fair," she said.

"All's fair, sweetheart." As if to prove that point, he hooked a hand around her neck and drew her into his kiss. Brief, bone-melting, breathtaking. Then he opened the back door and slung her bag inside.

"I have my bike."

"Tim took it home."

"Come again?" she said, stiffening. Incipient outrage chased away the shimmery warmth of his kiss. "Are you saying you *arranged* for my bike to be gone?"

He didn't deny it. In fact—smart man—he didn't say anything. He studied her quietly and then he touched a hand to her hair, threading a loose strand back behind her ear. "I'm sorry.

"Tim said whenever you needed to borrow his car he would take your bike." His thumb caressed the curve of her ear, and he shifted his weight, moving close enough that his breath warmed her forehead. "I wouldn't have made arrangements if I'd thought you would mind."

He sounded sincerely apologetic. Between his scent and his touch and the deep, earnest quality to his voice, Zara felt her irritation give and bow. She leaned into his touch and, maybe it was her imagination, but she swore she felt satisfaction in the smile he pressed to her forehead.

Damn him, he'd gotten his own way again. She was seeing a pattern here.

Eyes narrowed, she climbed into the car, pulled on her seat belt and waited. Once he'd joined her and angled the big vehicle onto the road, she turned to study him. "You're very used to arranging things to suit yourself, aren't you?"

One brow raised, he cut her a slow look. "You make that sound like a bad thing. What I'm doing is making things easier all around."

"For you."

"And for you."

That was what disturbed her about a relationship with Alex Carlisle. He tempted her to let him take charge. He weakened her resolve with a look, with a kiss, with a smile. He changed her mind as swiftly as a heartbeat, and made her lose control of her logic and her senses.

Last night she'd gone to dinner firmly resolved not to sleep with him. Then she'd convinced herself she deserved one night in his bed, one night of taking the pleasure and letting it fill the ache of loneliness that had felt more acute in the week since they'd met.

And then, in the bathroom this morning, he'd had his way again. She'd let him change her mind. She'd let him talk her into another night.

That weakness of willpower was all kinds of wrong.

Lost in her unsettling thoughts, she only realized he'd taken a left out of the car park a couple of blocks after the event. "Aren't we going back to your hotel?"

"No." His sideways glance was narrow, assessing. "We're going out of town."

That made her sit up straight, riled again by his high-handedness. "What if I have work tomorrow?"

"Do you?"

"I have to study."

"You have your books with you." He tipped his head to indicate her backpack. "Do you need others?"

"I…" Frowning, she let her breath go with a hiss of exasperation.

"Remember this morning when I asked you to spend the night with me?"

How could she not remember? Stunned after another shattering orgasm, from the tenderness in his face as he carried her into the shower, by the deep gravity of his voice when he asked.

"I remember," she said, her voice laced with those memories.

"You said you weren't that comfortable with five-star hotel suites. I decided we should spend tonight somewhere you would be comfortable." He kept his focus on the road and the city traffic as he switched lanes. "Do you want to go home to change? To get some more things?"

"Where are you taking me?"

A suppressed smile twitched at his mouth. "That's a surprise."

"You can't just pick me up and cart me off to God-knows-where," she said, trying for offended but sounding more intrigued than anything. Her heartbeat thickened. Where did he think she would be comfortable? How well did he think he knew her?

"I'm not abducting you."

"No?"

"Although I did think about it." His tone was conversational. The look he cast her wasn't. "Blindfolding you, taking a few wrong turns to throw your sense of direction off."

"No handcuffs? No tying me up?"

"We can still manage that…if you ask nicely."

Whew. His voice turned silky and the picture he painted

rippled through her, dark with erotic promise. Zara's nipples tightened sharply, and when she shifted in her seat, trying to ease the restless prowl of arousal, her camisole rasped against those hard points. She rolled her shoulders forward to ease the pressure. Saw him looking. Knew he knew he'd turned her on.

"No need to look so smug."

He laughed, a soft, dark sound that wasn't smug at all. "Don't worry, sweetheart. I turned myself on, too."

Okay, so that comment was just begging for her attention. Giving up on hiding her own reaction, she turned in her seat. Enough for her gaze to slide over him, touching the freshly shaven contours of his face and neck. The smoky-blue polo shirt, designer issue, natch. The hand he dropped from the wheel to rest lightly on his thigh, blocking her view of his lap.

Except then she got completely caught up in the slight tension in that hand, in the smattering of dark hair and the curve of muscle in his forearm. In the spread of his thighs against the car seat and the memory of them naked, thick and achingly male as they slid between hers, urging them apart, opening her to his first powerful thrust.

Omigod. She had to stop thinking about sex. She had to stop herself before she demanded he pull over, before she gave in to the wanton urge to reach out and touch the hard line she imagined inside those soft denim pants.

Before she caused a damn traffic accident.

Staring sightlessly through the windscreen, she breathed deeply until she'd centered herself. Her fingers, she noticed now, were curled tightly into the heels of her hands. Lucky she didn't have nails worth a razoo or she might have done herself an injury!

An awkwardness stretched in the silence, or maybe just

through her still-jangling hormones, and she felt she had to say something. The first thing that came to mind was, naturally, situated below his waist. "You're wearing jeans."

"Is this a problem?"

"No…just unexpected."

"I grew up wearing jeans."

In the outback. She kept forgetting that, blinded by the man in the suit or the exclusive designer casuals of last night. Even naked—and that's how she'd been picturing him a lot today—his first-class body was framed in sheets so soft, so fine, so exquisite, she'd been afraid they would melt under the heat of their joined bodies.

She'd forgotten last weekend and all the layers uncovered at the cabin.

Clarity snapped in her brain. That was it. How slow could she be in putting the clues together? His jeans. The four-wheel drive. A place he knew she enjoyed.

She whipped around, leaning into the center console. "You're taking me back to the cabin, aren't you?"

"Is that okay?" Their gazes met for a brief moment before his returned to the road. "You said it was your favorite place."

Wow. Yes. She probably had. But what stole her breath, tightening her chest and creeping beneath her defenses, was that he'd remembered. That he could have taken her anywhere—could have put her on his private jet and flown her anywhere in the world, most likely—but he'd chosen the simple. Her perfect place. That disturbed and delighted her in equal measures.

"I'm gobsmacked."

"Is that good?" he asked, and she might have imagined the hesitancy. The hint of uncertainty in his smoky gaze before it switched back to the front. "I thought you'd appreciate the quiet to study."

"What about you?"

"I can fish."

She probably gaped at him like an aquarium guppy. Luckily he was watching the road and didn't see. Quite simply, she couldn't picture him doing anything so restful. Despite the hidden layers. She remembered his pacing, prowling, unable to sit still for more than a few minutes that night at the cabin. "You fish?"

"Not in a long while," he admitted.

"I bet you haven't had a weekend off in a long while." When he didn't answer, Zara knew she was right.

"Did you bring work with you?" she teased, turning to peer into the back. Her attention snagged, not on a computer case or a briefcase, but on several boxes of camping supplies. Bedding. What looked like a stereo.

"Wow. You've come prepared."

"Impressed?"

No, she refused to be impressed by what he'd probably asked the hotel concierge to organize. "Are you trying to impress me?"

"Isn't that what first dates are all about?"

Is that what this was? A first date? Zara narrowed her eyes at him. "What was last night, then?"

He smiled, and the sideways look he cast smoked with meaning. Yet, somehow, despite that look of pure sex, he managed to keep his voice completely even, completely innocent, when he said, "That was just a meal. Remember?"

"In which case, I'm really looking forward to what you can do with a real date."

His laughter, rich with amusement, hot with promise, rolled over her and for a long minute she let herself tumble with it. Completely turned on. Completely unrepentant about wanting him and wanting to spend the rest of this weekend with him.

Later she could regret it. Later when, again, she would have to find the words to say goodbye.

Something in his expression shifted, stilling the laughter and thickening its warm resonance in her body. "What?" she asked, needing to know what that look was about.

"I was just thinking how beautiful you are."

And, yes, when he looked at her like that, she could almost believe him. Yet, instinct cautioned her to shake her head dismissively. He caught the gesture and didn't let it go.

"You have a beauty spot on your cheek." His gaze touched her there. "Another on your neck." And shifted to that spot, exposed by her open-necked shirt and her hair pulled back in a ponytail. "And then there's the third…"

On her breast. She felt his gaze lower, the stroke of heat, the sweet yearning for his hand, his mouth. The magic way he had with his tongue.

"Three proves it."

She shook her head, to clear the sexual heat. To counter with her own show of three. "My nose is too big. My face is too long. My teeth are too big."

"You have big teeth? Show me?" She bared them in a fake snarl and he laughed. "Sweetheart, you can bite me anytime."

"We can manage that…if you ask nicely."

Their eyes met again, a glancing slide of promise and anticipation that made Zara wish for the hotel suite. Any hotel suite. And then to decide that, no, she liked this teasing foreplay. The verbal sparring. The knowledge that she'd found a man—*a lover!*—with a clever mind and a clear focus.

A man she couldn't intimidate.

A man who'd vowed to protect her. Always.

"You need the left lane here," she said quickly, pointing out the sign off the freeway, and for several minutes he concentrated on crossing traffic and finding the road that wound into the Dandenongs. Young gums, as tall and straight and slender as supermodels, edged the road and Zara relaxed a little, imagining their calming eucalyptus scent in her nostrils.

Oh, yes, he had chosen well. She would enjoy tonight and tomorrow. She closed her eyes and—

"Tell me about your sister."

Damn. A dormant memory awakened suddenly to grab her by the throat. Last night, in bed, she'd murmured something about her sister and then she'd distracted him and distracted herself.

How could she have forgotten that slip? How could she have imagined that he-of-the-clever-mind would forget?

"She's my half sister, actually," she said. "Four months older than me, although she swears I act like the big sister."

"His legitimate daughter?"

"Yes." And without mentioning names, she told him how she'd met Susannah and how they'd become friends. How Susannah acknowledged their blood relationship when none of her family wanted to know, and how she'd promised to keep that relationship secret for the sake of her mother. "She's quite fierce about protecting her mother."

"I think I'd like your sister," he said, and Zara's heart thumped hard in her chest.

"I'm sure you would."

Hard as she tried, that statement did not come out level and free of irony. Breath held, Zara waited for him to comment, to stop looking at her in that puzzling way. In the end she couldn't stand the weight of the tension. "Why are you looking at me like that?"

"Trying to imagine how she could be more beautiful."

"Look, I'm not being precious about this beauty thing. I know I stand out in a crowd, but that comes with being an Amazon. People can't help but notice me." Frowning, she struggled to explain without even knowing why she needed to explain, why she couldn't just accept that this man found her beautiful and run with the lovely feelings that invoked. "I matured early. I can't remember a time when I wasn't the tallest in my class, but I wasn't always this lean, this fit."

"You worked hard at that?"

"I drove myself," she admitted, "after Mum got sick. I started running as a way of getting out in the open air for a while. Then I started to run to escape. Then I ran until it hurt."

"And when that didn't hurt enough, you took up kick-boxing."

She smiled tightly, acknowledging his astuteness. "I shouldn't have. It wasn't for the right reason."

"An aggressive release because your mother was hurting? Because you were hurting? What's wrong with those reasons? Better than having a breakdown from holding it all inside."

He would know, she realized, thinking about his mother. How she'd broken down from grief and the pressure of media hounding. They lapsed into silence for several minutes, several miles, and despite the aching sadness she always felt when remembering her mother's pain, Zara also felt a measure of comfort in knowing she could share this part of her life, so long held closely guarded, with another person.

How easy it was to share with him; how unexpected he was.

"She shouldn't have suffered so cruelly," she said softly,

the ache of remembered sadness thick in her voice. "No matter how hard I ran or how hard I punched and kicked, that never got any easier to take."

Zara woke with a start, surprised she'd relaxed enough to nod off in the passenger seat. Sitting up straight, she stretched the kink in her neck and the arm scrunched against the door handle and looked around.

They'd stopped. Her heart skipped a beat as she noticed where they had stopped. Her gaze zeroed in on the familiar outpost store and the couple she could see through the large front window. Alex, of course, looking tall and broad and heart-kickingly gorgeous in those jeans. He leaned against the counter watching Carmel, her mouth in nonstop motion, stack supplies into a large box.

A strong strand of emotion wound through Zara's chest. Instead of buying their food from an upmarket city deli, he'd taken a detour to give his business to someone who needed it more. To someone who'd done them a good turn.

In assuming he'd palmed off the details of this trip to a hotel concierge, she'd done Alex another disservice. He was so much more than she'd anticipated and for the first time this acknowledgment didn't ring cautionary alarms or cause stomach flips of anxiety.

For the first time she accepted that he could be more than her weekend lover. More than the man who'd awoken her dormant sensuality. This was a man she liked. A man to share her cares and concerns, her laughter and her tears.

She pressed a hand to her mouth, to still her burgeoning smile, but she couldn't suppress the knowledge that unfurled like a flower's petals in the morning sun.

This was a man she could love.

* * *

Unlike a week earlier, the evening was mild—warm enough inside the cabin that they could have done without a fire. Alex built one anyway. "So I can undress you in the firelight," he told her, and anticipation flared through Zara like a match to tinder.

He'd brought candles, too, and linen and crockery and fine crystal glasses.

"Your smooth side?" she asked, watching him pour wine. Watching the dance of candlelight and shadows over the raw angles of his face and thinking she would never describe him as smooth. He was too intense, too strong-minded, too male.

Naturally, he made a mockery of her judgment by producing the battery-operated stereo with all the flourish of a conjurer unveiling his best trick. He'd said a first date was all about making an impression. This, she knew, would be an impression that lasted a long, long time.

"You told me you liked to relax to music." The voice of a silver-tongued crooner drifted through the cabin as he held out her chair, inviting her to sit. "I wasn't sure what style."

"Bublé is a pretty nice choice. Very smooth. And considerably more romantic than knitting." She met his eyes across the table, letting him know she remembered that conversation. And that she appreciated him remembering.

"What has Carmel cooked up for us?"

A trout pâté, chicken, salad side dishes and freshly baked bread. Simple stuff, all beautifully prepared, all delicious. But how could she find room for food, when her appetite was all for the man sitting opposite her? The man who hadn't touched her since they'd left Melbourne. The man who watched her over the rim of his wineglass, his eyes lambent with the same desire that prowled through her blood.

The same restless energy that crackled in the air.

"Dessert?" he asked.

Zara shook her head.

"It's chocolate mousse."

"I know."

His nostrils flared. His eyes blazed with speculation as they drifted over her. "Take off your shirt."

Zara didn't bother with buttons. She simply lifted from the hem and peeled the shirt off. Underneath she wore a camisole, but it wouldn't have mattered if she'd worn nothing at all. She would still have stripped the shirt off.

"Only the shirt?" she asked.

"For starters." His voice was thick, low, aroused. She watched him sip from his wine and swallow. Felt the swell of response in her body, the tightness in her nipples, the ache of emptiness between her legs.

"Come over here."

She went without hesitation, her pulse a loud drumming of want in her ears. The blaze of heat in his eyes all the confidence she needed. Eyes locked on his, she took the glass from his hand and placed it on the table.

Then she straddled his lap and kissed him with all the pent-up hunger of a day without. He tasted of wine, rich and intoxicating. He turned her dizzy on the first sip, freed her ponytail on the second, stroked the length of her hair over her shoulders and breasts on the third.

Man, but he was some kisser.

"This is unexpected," he said when they came up for air. *This* was the silk camisole, one of the few pieces of sexy frippery she owned. He fingered the thin strap, the edge of lace across her breasts.

"Take it off," she whispered and he did.

But he didn't toss it aside. Instead he held it bunched in

his hand a second while his gaze glinted with wicked intent. Then he feathered it over her skin, tracing the slope of each breast, teasing her nipples into aching points.

Eyes closed, she arched her back into that gossamer touch. "I didn't take you for a tease."

He dragged the silky fabric over her again. "Doesn't that feel good?"

"Not as good as your hand." She stretched up straight and met his eyes. "Or your mouth."

His response, rough and hungry, growled in his throat.

Zara would have smiled with satisfaction but then his hand stretched wide on her back, pulling her to the strong, wet suction of his mouth, to all the magic he could do with her body, there in a straight-backed chair and on a linen-spread table amid the remains of their meal.

They didn't ever get to the mousse because he said he preferred the taste of her and he showed her how much, satisfying her cravings again and again, and it struck her in one dark molten aftermath that with Alex Carlisle in her life she might never need chocolate again.

They made love by the fireside, and in the midnight dark when she woke surrounded by his heat, and Zara wondered how many times she could come apart, how many times he could shatter her into tiny shards and then put her back together with the stroke of his hands and the blaze of those storm-blue eyes.

At some point she remembered asking him about almonds and he licked her throat and said, "That's what you taste of, sweetheart. Amber and honey and almonds," and she slept, too exhausted to tell him that was her perfume, a gift from her sister, as was the silk camisole.

A gift from Susannah, she thought as she drifted into sleep. Just like you.

Ten

She didn't study much, unless she counted studying Alex's very fine anatomy as they lazed in bed together Sunday morning. Alex didn't fish much, either, although they did take all the gear and trek down to Bad Barry Creek, mostly because he wanted to see her execute the specialist cast she'd bragged about over breakfast.

Relaxed and cocky, she almost slipped up telling him how she'd learned the skill.

"Pappy said it's all about feel and timing," she said as she commenced her forward cast, and he looked at her funny.

"I thought you said Susannah taught you."

Damn. She'd been quoting Susannah, but somehow in her memory she "heard" the instructions in the voice of her unknown grandfather. Ridiculous, but there it was. "Susannah's grandfather taught her," she covered smoothly. "I got used to her saying, 'Pappy said this, Pappy said that.'"

Which was the truth, after all.

She continued her demonstration but refining Alex's technique was another matter. She pointed out that his grip on the rod was too firm to make a smooth cast. He suggested she demonstrate on his rod—seeing as she'd mentioned the importance of choosing the right rod—and, well, things just deteriorated from there.

Later, they stretched out on the soft spring grass beside the stream, and Zara couldn't remember the last time she'd felt this relaxed, this carefree, this happy. She astounded herself by saying the words out loud.

"You want to stay relaxed and happy a bit longer?" Alex asked.

Nestled in the crook of his arm, Zara had to twist around to see his face. She could feel her heart fluttering just from looking into his sleepy eyes. Just from imagining what he might mean. "A bit?"

"Yeah." He grinned and tickled her bare belly with a blade of grass. "We could stay another night."

"What about work tomorrow?"

"We could play hooky."

She laughed softly and shook her head. "I can't imagine you playing hooky."

"You couldn't imagine me wearing jeans."

Point taken. Her gaze drifted down his body, relaxed, sated, not wearing jeans anymore. As always, her pulse picked up just by looking. "When did you last take a weekday off?" she asked.

"My father's funeral."

"For pleasure." But she pressed a kiss to his chest, not for pleasure but for comfort. Her unspoken message to say *I'm sorry you had to take a day off for that purpose.*

"I guess that would have been last November. Melbourne Cup day."

Zara snorted. "Half Australia takes Melbourne Cup day off. That does not count!"

"Have you ever been to the Cup?" he asked, conveniently changing the subject.

"No."

"I'll take you this year."

In five weeks' time? Her stomach tightened with longing but she didn't know how to respond, whether he was teasing, whether he was serious. His expression gave nothing away.

Wrinkling her nose, she chose the safe option. Light, teasing, dismissive. "I don't have a hat."

"So?"

"So, ladies have to wear a hat to the Cup. It's a rule!"

His brows dipped a fraction and she thought he was about to take issue with that rule. Then he reached over his head and retrieved the trucker's cap she'd been wearing earlier. Before he'd hauled it—and all her clothes—off her.

"There you go." He pulled it on her head, back to front. "A hat."

Amused by the mental image of an almost six-foot-tall woman strolling through the toffy Flemington members' enclosure wearing a pretty floral spring dress and a trucker's cap—especially on the arm of Alex Carlisle in one of his stylish Italian suits—she laughed long and hard. But then she caught a flash of emotion in his eyes, something that grabbed at her chest and squeezed all the air from her lungs and the laughter from her lips.

And there, lying beside an isolated mountain stream, naked but for a backward trucker's cap, she knew she'd gone and fallen in love.

Damn.

* * *

In the end, they didn't play hooky because Zara had a full day of lectures on Monday. *That's what really matters,* she reminded herself. *Your degree. The honors-year program. All-important exams in a month's time.* But when they arrived back in Melbourne Sunday evening and he asked, "Where to?" she couldn't bring herself to say *home.*

She spent another night in his hotel room, in his bed, and by the time she kissed him goodbye in the morning she'd convinced herself she could handle this affair. Driving back to the city, he'd repeated all the right things about not wanting promises or commitment. He wasn't going to be demanding. He lived in Sydney. He had the means to come and see her some weekends.

Others he would be too busy with work or travel.

Carlisle's international dealings took him away often, sometimes for a day or two, sometimes a week or more. Later this week he was flying to London to meet with U.K. executives, so she wouldn't see him for at least two weeks and that was okay. She would not let this euphoria of infatuation overwhelm her.

Surely, one day soon, she wouldn't grin like a loony every night when he called. Every time she heard "hello, Zara" in a voice as deep and dark as the late-night hour, she would not turn weak with longing.

She would not tell him she missed him. Absolutely not.

Over the next few days, she managed to keep her feet on the ground during the busy daylight hours. Whenever she found herself daydreaming about, say, spending the summer break in his Sydney harborside home or visiting his family's outback station, she gave herself a good mental shaking.

No promises, no commitment, remember?

She forced herself to remember that first weekend at the

cabin and their conversation about why he'd asked Susannah to marry him. He wanted a family; he was at that stage of his life.

Zara, most definitely, was not.

And thinking about that first weekend, about how they'd met, about Susannah, never failed to produce a twinge of guilt.

For a start, there was the whole sister-secret thing crouched like a dark phantom in the shadows, waiting to catch her out. She wanted to tell him—she *would* tell him—once she had Susannah's permission. Once she heard from Susannah who, apparently, was still in America.

During one of their long, late-night phone conversations, she asked Alex if he'd heard from her again. He hadn't.

"If she calls again, please get her number or ask her to ring me," Zara said. "I need to talk to her."

"Okay, but I doubt she'll call me."

"Why ever not?" And some inner demon reminded her that this was the woman he'd chosen as his wife. "What if she changes her mind about marrying you again?"

"She won't."

The certainty in his voice stilled her for a second. "Because of this other man? Does she love him?"

"I don't know. She said she'd never forgotten him; that she couldn't stop thinking about him. I said I understood."

Zara's heart started to thump so hard she barely heard the question she asked. "Do you?"

"Yes. That's exactly how I felt. About you."

Infatuation, not love, Zara cautioned herself afterward, but her heart didn't want to hear. It took off soaring and didn't touch down until later that week when a weekly gossip magazine hit the newsstands.

When she became front-page news as Alex Carlisle's "Mystery Melbourne Blonde."

* * *

She didn't even know until Tim brought the magazine home and tossed it on the kitchen table. "I talked to this dude on the phone, Zee. Twice." He picked up the magazine and studied it again, shaking his head accusingly. "You didn't say you were sleeping with a freakin' prince!"

He didn't notice Zara's face pale as she stared at the front page.

She hadn't seen a photographer. The series of pictures were obviously taken outside the Carlisle Grande last Friday night, after he'd taken her to dinner. Their clothes gave that away. So did their absorption in each other. The moment before the kiss. The kiss. Walking hand in hand into the hotel.

No need for any caption to say what was going on, she thought bitterly. It was all there on the front page.

How could she have been so stupid, so shortsighted, so oblivious? They'd talked about the media interest in his life, for Pete's sake. Why hadn't she paid attention? Why hadn't she realized?

A sick feeling clutched at her throat as she grabbed the magazine from Tim's hands and scanned the copy with swift eyes. *Mystery blonde…unknown beauty…latest lover.* No mention of her name, thank God.

She could feel the sheen of cold sweat on her skin as she slumped into a chair, weak and dizzy with relief.

"You all right, Zee?" Tim shifted uncomfortably, finally clued in to her distress. "You look like you've seen a ghost."

"Shock." She shook her head. Put down the magazine. Sucked in a deep breath. "I didn't know anything about this."

"You didn't know he was this 'Prince of the Outback' dude?"

"I knew that. I didn't think anything like this—" she waved a hand at the offending article "—might happen!"

"It's not that bad, is it? He's not married or anything."
Zara shook her head.

"And it's not like they're poxy photos. He caught your good side. Hey, you're even wearing a dress."

"Well, thank you, I think."

One of the things Zara liked about Tim was his sense of humor, and within five minutes he had her laughing at his Zara-as-Princess tomfoolery. By the time she traipsed upstairs to hit the books, she'd convinced herself that she'd overreacted.

She was only the mystery blonde. A five-minute fancy that wouldn't create any lasting interest because she wasn't a celebrity. They didn't know her background. They didn't know about her mother, right, so why should she worry?

Because one day they might find out, an inner voice whispered, *and then what?*

Alex didn't call that night and in a way she was glad. She needed perspective on the magazine piece, time to work out her true feelings, although none of that stopped her from sitting up past midnight in case the phone rang. Hours later she woke with a start, jackknifing upright in her study chair and spilling the remnants of her midnight milk all over her cytology notes.

Dumbly she stared at the mess, her heart racing from coming awake too quickly. From the horror of her dream. She grabbed a sweatshirt to sop up the milky puddle. In the bathroom she rinsed it clean and splashed water on her face, then rubbed at her eyes.

Nothing obliterated the nightmare front page stamped in her brain.

Mystery Blonde Exposed the headline screamed. The picture underneath was a sleazy pole dancer with her mother's face. The copy exposed Zara as the daughter of Ginger Love, former stripper and infamous mistress of transport tycoon Edward Horton. Illegitimate, unacknowledged, half sister of Alex Carlisle's former fiancée, Susannah Horton.

Weren't dreams supposed to be less overt? More open to interpretation?

Zara's sat cold and heavy in her mind and her stomach. A journalist would not have to dig too hard to come up with that front page. She'd never hidden her identity; she'd never felt any need to. She was simply a mature-age medical student, intent on making something of her life.

Linked with Alex Carlisle, she was all kinds of scandalous headlines, things he would not see coming.

Bracing herself on her forearms, she stared at her reflection in the bathroom mirror. Saw the churning ache of what she must do to reclaim her independence, her anonymity, her own identity.

She had to say goodbye.

Alex resisted the urge to push hard through his London meetings so he could fly home a day earlier. What difference would that make? He'd still be two days away from the weekend. Better he remain a full day's flying away from temptation, from this restless urge to see her sooner, to consign his take-it-slow declaration to hell.

Except, he had vowed to play it cool. To Zara and to himself.

He didn't want her ambushing his thoughts, night and day. He didn't like the ache of anticipation, waiting for the hours he knew he could call her at home. And he loathed the savage plummet of disappointment when all he got to hear was her short, perfunctory voice-mail message.

Zara here. Leave a message.

In the end he did leave a message. His contact number, instructions to reverse the charges, a couple of suitable times. And, because he couldn't help himself, a simple, sincere message.

"Call me, Zara. I miss talking to you."

But she didn't call him back and he hated the ensuing frustration more than everything else put together. He hated not knowing if she'd received his message. He hated the biting, gut deep worry that something might be wrong. And he hated the sense that he no longer controlled their relationship, that he might no longer control himself.

On Wednesday morning he arrived back in Sydney and headed straight to his office. And there, on his desk, on top of a stack of personal correspondence his PA had left for his perusal, he found her note. An innocent sheet of white notepaper, six neatly handwritten lines that turned his simmering frustration cold.

Alex read it again, searching for hidden meaning, feeling the cold turn to ice and the stab of each shard, word by word. Her message was clear: She'd reconsidered; she couldn't do a relationship; she was sorry.

Yes, she'd dressed it up in pretty words, words he'd heard before about not being the right woman for him, about not being able to handle the media attention he attracted, about how great that weekend had been but she believed they were better off to end it now.

Alex crumpled the note in his fisted hand and aimed it at the bin. He wasted half an hour pretending he could concentrate on work, pretending to listen to his PA's update, pretending he could deal with being cast aside as if that last weekend hadn't meant a thing.

As if she hadn't looked into his eyes and told him she'd

never been this happy, this satisfied, this contented. As if she hadn't told him on the phone, forty-eight hours later, her voice low and raspy with emotion, that she missed him already and wished he were there in her bed.

In her body.

He stood up abruptly, slapping the report file shut in the same single motion. "I'm going to Melbourne."

"Now?" To her credit Kerri's voice only rose slightly, although her eyes were wide with astonishment. Alex felt a sharp satisfaction. He wanted to shake things up. He needed to take control again. "When will you be back?"

"I have no idea," he said with grim determination. "But I sincerely hope it's not too soon."

Eleven

If Alex had stopped and thought this through, he'd have realized that finding Zara on a Wednesday might not be easy. If he'd employed a cool, calm, logical approach, he might have saved himself half a day of chasing his tail around Melbourne.

Not that he was chasing after Zara, exactly. His pride would not admit to that. He was chasing answers and some face-to-face honesty.

Except she wasn't at home. She wasn't answering her phone. She didn't have a client appointment until mid-afternoon. And finding her on campus proved an exercise in frustrating futility. As did sitting outside her empty Brunswick terrace on the off chance she arrived home.

By mid-afternoon when her personal training job was underway, Alex's temper crackled with impatience. It itched to surge through the door of the hotel gym, to interrupt her session five minutes in, to demand her time and her attention and her explanation.

Only the heat of that impulsive urge held him back. He'd spent too many years learning to control himself, to countermand that heat with cool control, not to recognize the danger signs. So he waited out the whole hour, waited until her client, red-faced from exertion, came out the door and headed for the elevators.

Then he slowly got to his feet and walked into the small gym.

She was alone. That's all he noticed in the first twenty seconds. That and the wide flare of her eyes when she turned and saw him standing just inside the doorway. Her mouth formed a silent word of surprise—possibly his name—and then she drew herself taller and attempted a smile.

"I didn't know you were back," she said around that fake smile, "let alone in town."

"Why would you? You didn't return my call."

"Your...call?"

Her breath caught in the middle of her question as he started toward her. Six slow, deliberate steps that brought him close enough to see the guarded expression in her eyes. To see the beat of elevated pulse in her throat. "Didn't you get my message? From London?"

"Yes, but with the time difference..."

"You couldn't find five minutes that might have worked for both of us?" Alex forced himself to speak evenly, coolly, conversationally. "So you decided a note would be enough. Is that a trick you learned from Susannah?"

Her gaze snapped back to his. Shock radiated from their depths. "No. I'm sorry, Alex. I did try to call and then—"

"Forget it," he cut in, hating that he'd exposed himself to her sympathy with the reminder of Susannah's note.

"The thing about notes," he continued even more dispassionately, "is what's left out. What's open to interpretation."

"You didn't think my note was clear enough?"

"Oh, your message was clear enough. It was nice while it lasted. Goodbye."

She pressed her lips together and looked away, and Alex set his jaw against the simmer of his temper.

"Did you consider who might read that note? Did you think that my PA might open all my mail?"

That brought her gaze whipping back to his. "Your PA read my note? When I marked the envelope as personal?"

The sharp rise of her voice, the irritation in her eyes, snarled mean knots in his mood and all he could think was *Good.* He wanted her mad. He wanted an argument.

"Yes, she read it," he said tightly. "Yes, she knows I'm the best sex you ever had."

Color flared along her cheekbones. "I did not say that!"

"You inferred it." And it gave him no satisfaction at all, he discovered as she turned away to pick up her gym bag from the floor. None at all. "Don't worry. I pay Kerri enough money. She's not about to tell the world."

Bag in hand, she straightened. "The world already knows."

Alex stiffened, his attention snared by her comment and the odd note of resignation in her voice. By the sudden bolt of understanding that tightened the muscles in his shoulders and back and jaw. "Was there something in the papers while I've been away?"

She nodded. "Last week. Front page of *Goss.*"

Damn. "Photos?"

"Outside the hotel. And going into the hotel." Her mouth twisted into a smile that didn't take. "I was your mystery blonde for two days and then a couple of the weekend papers ran my name in their society gossip column."

"And this is when you decided we were over?" he asked slowly. His heart beat harder, lacing his blood with a new optimism. *This* was an answer. *This* he could understand. "Because of a magazine that isn't worth the paper it's printed on?"

"I don't want someone taking my photo when I know nothing about it. I don't want to be on any front pages. I don't care which magazine or which paper." There was a fierceness in her voice he'd heard before, over breakfast at Carmel's café when she'd told him about her mother's exposure to the media.

When he'd sensed a strong connection because they'd understood each other.

"Not even a medical journal?" he asked, letting her know he remembered that conversation.

"I'm talking about being on the front page for no reason other than being your lover."

Hurt and regret and something else shimmered in her eyes and Alex couldn't stop himself from reaching for her, to hold her, to reassure her. But she hugged her gym bag to her chest like a barricade. A clear sign that she didn't want him any closer.

"If it was only me on the magazine cover I wouldn't care quite so much," she continued. "But last week it was an anonymous blonde and then it was Zara Lovett and next time it will be Stripper's Daughter and they'll find photos of Mum and run them next to yours."

"And you think…what? That I'll be shocked to find out your mother was a stripper?"

She frowned. Hugged her bag even closer. "You knew?"

"No, and I don't care." He started to reach for her again, but she flinched before he got within six inches. "I don't care what the papers say, Zara. I told you that."

"You told me you care when it hurts other people."

This time he didn't let her pull away. He took her by the shoulders and held her still and forced her to meet his eyes. "What did the magazine say, Zara? How did it hurt you?"

"Not me, my mother. I don't want her name and her memory dragged through the muck."

"You would rather walk away? From this? From us?"

"I would rather walk away now," she said softly, but her gaze was strong and sincere. "Before we get any more involved. Before they start digging for dirt."

"I don't care—"

"You *do* care, Alex, and that's the thing. This isn't only about me or you or us, and it's not even just my mum. You said your mother hates the media muckraking. Don't you see?" She let go of the bag, let it drop to the floor beside her with a thick thud, and then her hands were on his, giving them a little shake as if that might jostle his obdurate stance. "They'll drag up Mum's old story from the archives and then they'll jump onto your mother's, too. They'll have a field day rehashing those old scandals, all the juicy details, all the lies. The heartache. I couldn't stand that and I know your family couldn't either.

"I'm sorry, but I just…I just can't!"

The husky ache in her voice gripped Alex by the throat, turned his voice sharp and harsh. "So, you're taking the coward's way out and giving up? Would that make your mother proud?"

Her head reeled back as if he'd struck her. "Yes," she said distinctly after a second. "Yes, she would be proud that I'm unselfish. That I'm thinking about the other people this would hurt."

"I'll look after my mother's concerns."

"And what about my father's family? What about his widow? She won't want to see her husband's cheating affair rehashed again and for what? So we can have a good time between the sheets whenever we can find time!"

"Is that how you see our relationship?"

"What else is it, Alex?"

He stared into her face, into the resolute darkness of her eyes, and felt all the frustration of the long day return tenfold. *Damned if he told her all he wanted to; damned if he didn't.*

But he had to keep trying. He wasn't nearly ready to let her go. "It's nothing if you give in to the guttersnipes. If you let them run your life and rule your decisions. We're nothing if you toss what we have aside without giving it a chance."

"I have to. I'm sorry."

"Are you? Or is this a convenient out?"

A spark of heat lit her eyes and for a second he thought he might yet get a chance to argue hot and strong. But with a slow expulsion of breath she banked the fire.

"It doesn't matter why, does it? Just…let me go. I have to shower and change. I've got a study date."

Zara knew she'd made a mistake using the *date* word. She saw his eyes narrow, saw the twitch of a muscle in his jaw just before she ducked down to scoop up her bag.

But she hadn't expected him to follow her into the ladies' locker room.

Intent on keeping her legs moving forward, on not buckling to the urge to turn around, to go back for one last kiss, she hadn't even heard him follow. Not until the door shut behind her with a firm snap. As if propelled by a hand.

She swung around. Her gasp sounded way too loud in the tiny room, as if it bounced off the white tile walls and came back at her from all directions, amplified a hundred times. "What are you—" Her throat was tight, her voice so faint that she licked her lips and tried again. "What are you doing?"

His gaze rolled from her lips to her eyes. His, she noted with a spike in her pulse, were no longer cool. No longer contained. "A study date?"

"In half an hour." Pleased her voice had regained strength, she flung her bag on the bench and folded her arms across her chest. "So I'd appreciate if you left me to get ready."

"This won't take long."

"To walk back out that door? No, that won't take long."

She crossed to the single shower enclosure and turned on the taps as far as they would go. Hot water gushed, a stream of liquid sound, a statement of her intent. *Conversation closed, Alex Carlisle. Now leave.*

But as she returned to her bag, she heard the snick of the lock catching and her gaze jolted back up. "You locked the door? What are you doing?"

"Ensuring we're not disturbed."

Zara was gripped by an insane urge to laugh. The sound of that door locking disturbed her. *He* disturbed her with the way he watched her through the gathering cloud of steam.

Predatory intent, narrow, sharp, purposeful, flitted across his expression and Zara felt a frisson of alarm in her skin. And deeper, in her flesh and the female core of her body, a much stronger bolt of anticipation and heat and all the things she should not be feeling.

Damn him. Why couldn't he make this easy? Why couldn't he accept that she couldn't have a relationship with him?

Because then he wouldn't be the man he is, her inner voice of honesty retorted. *You wouldn't have fallen for him. You wouldn't be locked in this room with him, dreading his next move and craving it in the same breath.*

She had to stay firm. She had to keep him at arm's length. She had to convince him that she meant no.

"Alex, there's nothing else to say. Please, will you just accept that?"

"I wish I could. It would make my life a hell of a lot easier."

"Then try harder," she countered.

But he'd started toward her, his eyes as fiercely insistent as his voice. "I can't, Zara."

Zara had nowhere to go, no escape from the man or from the awareness that engulfed her more hotly, more surely, a thousand times thicker than the steam swirling from the shower.

She didn't know she'd been backing up until she hit the wall, until he stopped right in front of her, his hands flattened on the tiles on either side of her head.

"Don't," she breathed.

"Don't?"

"Don't touch me."

His eyes narrowed. "I'm not."

Technically, he was right. But he stood so close she could feel the heat rolling off his body in stark counterpoint to the cold tiles at her back. When their eyes clashed she felt the jolt of electricity course through her veins. Felt the tingle in her breasts.

Oh, the danger. This much electricity in a wet room spelled doom.

Zara tried to shrink back farther, away from the sparks, away from the temptation. She saw the corners of his mouth tighten and knew she had about a second to regain the ascendancy.

"You're not touching me. Fine. Then what do you want?" she asked on a note of desperation. "What is your point?"

He stared at her a moment and she had the distinct impression he didn't know. That he'd acted on impulse, instinct, perhaps on thwarted pride. Because the way she'd done it—the note and the media exposé reason—punched his hot buttons and because he'd had enough of women leaving him.

"Is it because I wrote you a note?" she asked, against her better judgment. "Is that why you won't accept that I meant every word of it?"

"Perhaps I need to hear it again." His voice as soft as the billowing steam, he leaned infinitesimally closer. So close that each word stroked her skin with the sweet warmth of his breath. "Tell me you don't want me, Zara. Tell me you don't ache for me, that what I'm seeing in your eyes isn't the burn you're feeling in your blood."

"Don't do this, Alex," she whispered. "Don't use sex to try and manipulate me."

He stilled. She felt his tension like a renewed blast of heat. "Is that what you think I'm doing?"

"Yes!" *Damn him.* And a sudden burst of anger came to her aid. Straightening, she met his gaze full on. "You came in here and locked the door. You stalked over here and trapped me against this wall after I asked you to leave. You knew you only had to get close to manipulate this chemistry we have—"

He slapped his hand down on the tile beside her head so hard she recoiled. For a second he just stared into her eyes and what she saw there, the seething, burning heat, shocked her into action. With both hands, she pushed at his chest until he ceded several inches.

"Do you really think that's all this is? Chemistry?"

"Yes," she said with quiet intensity. "And I can't deal with that kind of stuff. It's too much."

"Do you think I like it? Do you think I want to feel like I'm—" He stopped abruptly, eyes blazing in his tightly drawn face. "Hell, Zara. In your note you said it was great. Your best time ever."

Her heart wailed a protest, but she lifted her chin and refused to listen. It didn't matter what she felt because she couldn't have him. He was the pain and the dread of front-page revelations. He was a man used to getting his way, a man not used to compromise. Ridiculous that she'd thought they could work out some basis for a long-distance relationship.

Ridiculous that she'd considered he could be her man, her soul mate, her love.

Abruptly he swung away, slamming a hand through his hair in a gesture of abject frustration. But he turned back just as quickly, fire still blazing in those razor-sharp eyes. "What do I have to do to change your mind, Zara? Do I have to ask you to marry me? Will that make you reconsider how much I want you?"

"Marry you?" she repeated, her eyes wide with disbelief.

And then she started to laugh, an edgy stop-start sound that did nothing to soothe the roar in Alex's ears and in his blood. The temper he so badly needed to control.

He turned away, focused on an irritant he could control. The damn shower still spraying at full blast. Quickly he strode over, reached into the enclosure and shut it down.

"You find that funny?" he asked, turning back around.

As quickly as it had started, her laughter shut down too. "That wasn't amusement. That was astonishment."

Which she hardly needed to state. Alex saw it in her eyes, in the soft set of her mouth. Stunned, yes, but also taken aback by his uncharacteristic outburst.

"Nothing will change my mind or anything else about this situation. Including any other temper tantrum you might be thinking of throwing."

Her calm words hit him with the cold dose of realization he needed. He'd almost lost it. Like some spoiled rich kid denied his candy.

You can't always have what you want.

Hell.

He'd almost let passion and frustration override his usual cool counsel and that shamed him and horrified him and scared him in equal measures.

"You're right, of course," he said stiffly. "It seems you bring out the best in me and the worst in me."

"I'm sorry, Alex."

He met her eyes and knew she'd slipped away as surely as the rapidly dissipating steam. Knew there was nothing he could do to keep her. "Not half as much as I am."

Zara didn't have anything else to say because there was nothing left to say. Her expression as rigid as her posture, as tight as the cloying atmosphere in the tiny room, she watched him turn and walk out the door without any word of goodbye. And that was okay. Her emotions did not need any further battering.

And when he was gone, she expelled one long, broken breath and got on with what had to be done.

She showered, she dressed, she got herself to her study session and forced her mind to participate at some remote automated level. She kept it all together until later that night when Tim wandered into her room and flung himself on her bed, as he was wont to do when he needed a break from study.

He took one look at her face and asked who'd died.

A tightness grabbed the back of Zara's throat and, dammit, she felt the raw burn of tears. "PMS," she muttered.

"Ah, The Hormones," Tim intoned with suitable gravity. Then, bless his heart, he fetched her two Tim Tams from his secret stash and the chocolate cured her ridiculous urge to cry.

For the moment.

Over the next few days, she resorted to the chocolate fix frequently and unrepentantly. This breakup—and, okay, she'd only met Alex three weeks ago but their connection had been so intense, it felt like much longer—could not have happened at a worse time.

Her hormones were doing a crazy dance with her emotions. She wasn't sleeping well and the pressure of approaching exams and of watching the papers every day with a sick feeling they may yet pounce on her mother's story or her relationship with the late, esteemed Edward Horton, had delayed her period.

That had happened before. She wasn't worried; she was just…stressed. They'd had sex—a lot of sex—that weekend but they'd always used condoms.

And thinking about that, about the powerful pleasure of making love with Alex, did not help her insomnia.

Hands fisted in her pillow, Zara squeezed her eyes shut tighter against the memories and the tide of longing that rose swift and strong. This was the part she hated most. The doubts that swelled in the dark of night, in the hours when she felt her loneliness most, when her heart asked why she hadn't admitted her feelings when he'd given her the chance.

In the light of day, the answer came all too easily.

Why admit she loved him when they had no future? One day she did want love, commitment, marriage, but with a man she could spend the rest of her life alongside. One she could be honest with about every aspect of her past. One she would have gladly taken home to meet her mother, Ginger Love, stripper and scarlet woman.

She could not see Alex Carlisle in that role.

Besides, the marriage thing had been an expulsion of his frustration. A taunt rather than a proposal. Imagining they could make a marriage work because they had great sex was ludicrous. Her life plan was based around finishing her interrupted degree. That's what mattered to her.

She'd worked her butt off to keep up the distinction average needed for a shot at next year's honors program. She couldn't blow it now. She couldn't allow the distraction of Alex Carlisle to encroach upon her study time.

He was gone, done, over.

During the next week, she trained herself not to jump whenever the phone rang. Forced herself to stop checking the door of the gym every session in case he suddenly appeared. And because this was driving her nuts, she told the Personal Best receptionists not to give out her schedule or whereabouts to anyone—*anyone!*—without her approval.

But he didn't call or try to contact her.

This is good, Zara told herself, as she paid for her purchase and strode out of the campus pharmacy. Her stomach churned with anxiety and she gripped the paper package more tightly. Outside she paused—she had to pause because she suddenly felt a bit dizzy. Light-headed.

"Are you all right?"

"Yes. Thank you," Zara said, recovering. And when she looked around at the woman who'd expressed concern, her eyes widened in recognition.

So did Professor Mark's. "Zara! I haven't seen you in months and now today of all things peculiar!"

"Why is today peculiar?" Zara asked before she could stop herself.

Her favorite professor, her mentor through the tough first semester when she'd resumed study, smiled. "Oh, I've just come from a meeting where we were discussing some of the honors candidates for next year." She pursed her lips. "No guarantees, you understand, with this year's finals still to come. But there is a short list."

Zara's heart lurched and raced, but she didn't whoop and yell. She did smile very broadly. "I understand. Of course."

They talked a little more about how she was managing her course load before going their separate ways. Zara's stride bounced with elation. No guarantees, but she was short-listed.

All she'd aimed for, all she'd strived toward, was within her grasp. All she had to do was keep up her study schedule so she performed in her exams next month.

Smiling like a fiend, she punched the air with her fist…and came back to earth with a dizzying thud. Her fingers tightened on the little bag in her hand and her stomach lurched sickly.

Okay, she told herself, sucking in a deep breath. No need for alarm. This test is just in case. To eliminate the likelihood. To stop the clutches of night panic.

All the way home she dealt with her gathering nerves by refusing to accept the possibility. She could not be pregnant. Fate could not be so cruel.

Half an hour later, she sat on the edge of the bathtub and the bottom fell out of her world.

She stared at the distinct second line on the stick, compared it again with the control band and with the instructions, and accepted the inevitable.

Fate could be that cruel.

She was pregnant.

Twelve

She had to tell Alex, but after the disastrous episode with the note, Zara was leery about how. In her heart she knew this deserved face-to-face—in her heart, she *wanted* to tell him face-to-face—but the logistics defeated her. She couldn't jump on a plane and go to Sydney. Not when she was having trouble jumping out of bed each morning.

And therein lay the biggest logistical problem.

As if triggered by the appearance of that second pink line, morning sickness had struck instantly. She wasn't completely debilitated, just severely limited. And tired. And anxious about how long this would last and how many lectures she would miss and how this might affect her ability to concentrate for her upcoming exams.

Yup, a trip to Sydney was out of the question, which meant she would have to ask Alex to come and see her. That provided her next challenge. A dozen times she'd composed her side of the conversation. Two or three times she got as far as picking up the phone.

But the thought of asking him to come and see her without telling him why, imagining him jumping to several different conclusions and insisting on the full story over the phone, never failed to churn her stomach into a new bout of nausea.

If only she could pick the perfect time to leave a message on his voice mail. That seemed like the perfect, simple solution. She'd started working on the message.

Hello, Alex. This is Zara. I need to see you. It's rather important. When you're next in Melbourne could you give me a call?

At which point, she would see the flaw in her perfect, simple plan.

He would have to call her back to arrange the meeting. He would want to know why, and she didn't want to blurt out, "I'm pregnant," in a tense, overheated telephone conversation.

She wanted…oh, gads, she didn't know what she wanted.

When she wasn't being sick or recovering from being sick or worrying over her life falling apart, she teetered between fear and burgeoning wonder. A baby. Would she be able to manage all the change and the challenges that entailed? Would she make a good mother, the kind a child could laugh with and learn from and love with all their heart?

Oh, she hoped so. She'd had the best example. And then she would think of Alex and his part in her baby's life and worry would pitch her stomach again.

She recalled his strong opinion on two-parent families, their heated debate the night of the storm, his reasons for wanting to marry Susannah.

And she could not bring herself to pick up the phone.

Next week, her newly discovered inner coward whispered. *Next week you might be handling the morning sickness better and next week he might be in Melbourne for the races and you can leave a message saying you'll meet him at his hotel at a specific time.*

A decent plan. Better than decent, really, because she wasn't asking him to fly down here specially. Except then she remembered him joking about taking her to the races in her trucker's cap, which made her remember him undressing her beside the mountain stream and tossing the cap aside.

She remembered how he'd looked at her when he pulled the band from her ponytail and let her hair fall around her face. How he whispered the word *beautiful* over and over when she came apart beneath his body.

And tears clogged her throat because she knew they could never regain the magic of that weekend. Not with the complications of an unplanned pregnancy and all kinds of compromises and decisions to be made.

Then, the day before the Melbourne Cup, her plan backfired.

Tim was studying the form guide, pretending that might help him pick the winner. Since this was the only horse race and only form guide he ever looked at, year to year, Zara sincerely doubted it. She was studying histology and paying no attention to his occasional muttered comment.

Until she heard the magic word.

She swung around, staring over the top of her reading glasses. "Did you say Carlisle?"

"His horse is scratched. Tough break," he added, with no sympathy whatsoever. Although he continued to read out the newspaper piece about Irish Kisses, Zara barely listened.

All she could think was: his horse isn't running; there goes my plan.

"When are you going to tell him?"

Tim's quiet question twined through her thoughts and she sighed heavily. "I thought he'd be in town for the races. I was planning on seeing him tomorrow."

"There's always the phone," he said after a pause. "In case you hadn't thought of that."

"I'm still working on what to say."

Tim snorted. "Call him now, Zee. Don't think about it. Just pick up the phone and do it."

"Tomorrow," she decided, turning back to her books, and her inner coward breathed a sigh of relief at the reprieve. "I'll call him tomorrow."

Alex didn't want to be in Melbourne. It might be a big city, one he loved for its racing and its restaurants and its people, but now his mind only conjured up one of those people. Zara. As soon as his jet landed, he felt a new tension in his muscles and an edginess in his veins.

He wasn't going to see her. She'd made her feelings perfectly clear on his last visit and he sure as hell didn't need to haul his pride through those hot coals again.

That same bruised pride wouldn't allow him to call off his Melbourne Cup trip, either. Despite the disappointment of Irish's injury, he wanted to be at the track on Australia's biggest race day. It was a tradition and he supposed at some level a test.

Go to Melbourne, Alex. Prove to yourself you can spend two nights and a day in the city without tracking her down.

Well, here he was. One night down and this morning he hadn't given in to the temptation of calling Personal Best and booking her for a training session. And, yeah, he was man enough to admit that he had been tempted.

"Masochist," he muttered, shaking his head.

Instead of facing memories he'd as soon forget in a hotel gym, this morning he'd swum. Exercise for his body and to clear his head from a late night at the Cup Eve Ball. He showered, he dressed, and while he had coffee he checked for messages with the hotel and then on the phone he'd not taken with him last night.

When he got to the last of the voice-mail messages, everything inside him stilled.

"Um. This is Tim Williams. In Melbourne. Zara's housemate. I, uh…can you call me…if you get this message tonight?"

The voice paused, then came back with a phone number. Alex didn't bother writing it down. He knew it by heart. And all he could think was that something must be wrong.

Why else would her housemate call?

He started punching in the number. Then stopped and closed his phone. Tim had asked him to call last night. On a Tuesday morning he would probably have already left for classes.

And if he was home?

Alex reached for his suit jacket and started for the door.

If he was home, then Alex would soon know why he'd called.

If she started the day slowly, if she ate some dry cereal in bed before moving at all, if she concentrated on relaxation and not on that wasted first hour, Zara's morning sickness was bearable and she could function for the rest of the day. Skip any of those steps and the first wasted hour could stretch to two, three, or right through the rest of the day.

Today she'd woken too early and after too little sleep,

already anxious over the phone call she'd vowed to make and with no bedside snack. Three strikes and with no one to blame but herself. Shivering from however long she'd spent on the cold bathroom floor, she crawled back into bed and closed her eyes.

Half an hour, she thought weakly. I just need thirty minutes to gather the strength to go downstairs and eat. To dress and get to the university.

She must have slept. She didn't remember nodding off but she woke with a foggy head and a dry mouth and a surprisingly steady stomach. When she turned her head and saw the mug and bowl on her bedside table, she managed a feeble smile.

"Tim, you are a sweetie."

Moving slowly to guard her precious equilibrium, she sat up and started the breakfast he'd left. Dry cereal and raisins. Tea gone cold. And suddenly it wasn't her physical or gastric stability at risk, but her emotional calm. Tears thickened her throat until she couldn't swallow and she had to cradle her mug in both hands to stop it shaking.

Damn, damn, damn.

She hated these debilitating, emotional jags that waylaid her at the least provocation. This one because of Tim's thoughtful gesture. And because he'd remembered what she'd forgotten and because her prized self-sufficiency was as shaky as her hands and because she didn't know how much longer this would go on and because she hated feeling incapacitated, weak, reliant.

And because, she realized as the tears brimmed and started to roll down her cheeks, she would likely lose Tim as a housemate and surrogate brother. How could he stay and study with a baby crying through the night? How could she keep this house with its steep stairs and temperamental heating? Where would she be in twelve months and how would she be managing?

Gripping her mug a little tighter, she controlled the fretful tears by thinking about what she needed to do. She had to start making decisions, thinking about her future and all the changes this would bring.

Today she would call Alex. Today it would start.

With renewed resolve, she finished her breakfast. She wouldn't rush to try and make her nine o'clock lecture. She needed to let the food settle. Then she would shower and dress. She could be out the door by—

Above the muted music downstairs she heard the leaden rap of their front-door knocker. Her pulse lurched, for no good reason, and she rolled her eyes at herself.

It isn't him. It can't be him.

Still that didn't halt the prescient quiver that snaked up her spine.

The knocker sounded again and she put down her mug. Carefully, since her hand was shaking again. Perhaps Tim had already left. Often he did that, waltzing out the door without turning off the radio or the lights or his computer.

She started to swing her legs out of bed and then stilled—everything stilled—when she heard the distinctive creak of the front door opening. And voices. Tim's droll drawl and a deeper, stronger pitch that sent her recently subdued emotions into another fever pitch of turmoil.

Alex was here. Downstairs. In her home.

And she was about to lose her breakfast.

Another minute. Alex eyed the door of the front room where Tim had left him waiting, pacing, putting his patience through the wringer. He eyed the door but he pictured the stairs in the narrow hallway beyond, the stairs he'd heard the housemate bound up at least five minutes ago.

Another minute and then he'd…what? Go and find her for himself? Force her to see him, when the message delivered by her nonappearance was as clear as the scowl on his face? As loud as the female rocker screeching on the radio in the room next door?

Alex paced another round of a room not designed for pacing. He'd tried sitting, on the bright red sofa that dominated the tiny room, but he'd sunk so deep that the cushions heaped all over the thing had spilled into his lap. And then he'd heard the sound of running water upstairs and he'd sprung to his feet in an instant.

She hadn't appeared then. She hadn't appeared since.

What the hell was he doing here anyway?

Yes, Tim had called. But when he answered the door this morning, he'd looked sheepish and ill at ease. "Look, man, I might have overstepped, y'know"

"You did call about Zara?"

Tim had scratched at his chin and winced. "Sort of. I didn't expect you'd call in person."

"Is she home?"

"Yeah, but she's still in bed."

"Is she sick?" he'd bit out instantly, remembering the morning at the cabin. Remembering her languid stretch and her guilty grin when she admitted she never slept in. "Is that why you called?"

"She's, um, a bit off color. Look, why don't you come in and I'll see if she's up yet."

Running water and every screaming instinct told Alex she was up, but avoiding him. His pride suggested he take the hint and leave. But then he heard footsteps in the hall outside and he whipped around just as the door opened.

He saw her and didn't see her; felt too much, too swiftly, to take in anything except the fact that she was here, and he still wanted her more than his next breath.

Then she flipped back her hair, loose, no ponytail, and that simple action steadied his first rush of response, focused his gaze on the woman who stood in the doorway looking gaunt and pale and still.

Realization hit him like a tidal wave, knocking the breath from his lungs, sucking the sand from under his feet. Slowly his gaze dipped to her waist and he heard the intake of her breath and saw the flutter of nerves in her hand the second before she pressed it to her flat stomach.

Reflexive, protective, and more revealing than any words.

"When were you going to tell me?" His gaze rolled back to her face. "Or weren't you going to bother?"

Her eyes widened slightly, hurt, shocked. "Of course I was—"

"When?"

"Today. I was going to call you today."

Right. "And that's why your housemate felt he should intercede?"

Her lips tightened visibly. "Tim thought he was doing me a favor."

"Yes. He was."

For a second he just stared at her, battling a barrage of conflicting emotions. At the moment anger was ahead on points and she must have read that on his face and in his body language because she sucked in a breath and lifted her chin a little. "Please, Alex, can we not do this now? I can't—"

"You want me to come back later? You want me to walk away and go about my business after finding out you're pregnant?"

"No," she said in cool, clear contrast to the rising heat in his voice. "I want you to understand that I'm not up for a fight. Sorry, but if that's what you want then you will have to come back another time."

Their eyes met, clashed and he felt a gut-punch of remorse. "You look like hell."

"You noticed?"

And that one wry question wiped away his anger, wiped away everything but a powerful wave of protective concern. "How long have you been sick? Have you seen a doctor? Isn't there something they can give—"

"Slow down. Just…sit down." She waved a hand toward the sofa. "I'll make some tea."

Alex set his jaw. "I don't want tea. I want answers."

"Well, I do want tea, as it happens." She pressed a hand to her stomach again and he was struck again by how thin she was. "And another breakfast."

"You've lost weight."

"I dare say."

How could she be so blasé? This was her health, the baby's health. *His* baby's health! "Dammit, Zara, sit down. I'll make you tea and…what can you eat?"

Too wrung out to object, Zara let him feed her. Sitting at the kitchen table, she gave him directions on what to make, where to find things, and tried to focus on how small and shabby he made her kitchen look, with his elegant navy suit and red silk tie and perfect grooming. Focusing on the superficial and reassuring him about her health—several times—helped keep her trepidation down to a dull roar.

But then, while she ate, he leaned against the counter and watched. He was so quiet, so cool, that for a second she wished back the dark slice of anger he'd displayed earlier. At least that was an emotion she understood.

This Alex was infinitely more dangerous because she didn't know how he'd strike and therefore she couldn't prepare to defend. And if he kept watching her like that, if her stomach kept churning with her rising anxiety, then she wouldn't have to worry about anything except making the bathroom in time.

"How did this happen?"

Zara looked up from spreading a second slice of toast. She didn't know that she wanted to eat a second slice, but she liked having something to do. She liked the cool and solid strength of the knife in her hand, too. Not so much a defense as a prop.

"The pregnancy?" she asked, meeting his eyes. Resisting the smart-mouth answer that sprang to mind. "Well, you were there."

"We used protection. Every time."

Oh, yes. So many times, so many ways. All of them completely mind-blowing.

Zara looked back at her toast, away from the heat of that thought reflected in his darkening eyes. Away from the flare of color along his cheekbones. The look she'd seen so many times when he came to her after donning protection. Or while she'd rolled it on, slowly, carefully, tormenting and teasing.

The knife clattered from her hand, breaking that dangerous thread of thought.

"Condoms don't offer one hundred percent protection." She adopted a practical, professional tone. "For various reasons, but mostly user error."

He didn't say anything for a long moment but she felt his tension, felt it stretching between them like a physical entity. "Did you know the last time I was in Melbourne?"

Zara shook her head. "I would have told you if I'd known. I know how important this is to you."

"You're going to have the baby?"

"Of course I am! What did you think?"

"I don't know. You haven't given me the chance to think."

Oh, but that hurt. The words and the insinuation, the cool tone and the spark of accusation in his eyes. "You know, it came as something of a shock to me, too. I've had a lot to think about and to deal with—"

"Dammit, Zara, I could have shared all that!" He rocked forward off the counter, as if he couldn't maintain that fake-casual stance any longer. "I could have been looking after you, getting you medical care, making sure you were eating properly."

"I hope you're not implying I've been neglectful."

"How can you look after yourself here?" He waved a hand around. "Alone? With your study and your work. You look like—"

"Hell, I know. You have pointed that out."

And somehow they were back at glaring odds, except this time the anger simmered just as strongly in Zara. How dare he imply that her home—bought with her mother's estate, her only asset, and perfectly adequate for her needs— wasn't good enough?

How dare he imply that she couldn't look after herself and her baby?

Instinctively, her hand dropped to her lap. "I have been looking after myself," she said coolly, "since before I turned twenty. For four of those years I also nursed my mother through a debilitating illness. I'm a medical student and I know how to protect my health."

His look suggested otherwise but he didn't say so. He

didn't say anything for a long, tense moment. Then he blew her right away. "I want to marry you, Zara. As soon as we can make arrangements."

Zara sucked in a breath but it wasn't enough to stop the giddy whirl in her brain. "You want to marry me? Because I'm pregnant?"

"Because we're going to have a baby together. Yes."

"I…" Her voice trailed off. She licked her lips and tried again. "I don't see how that would work."

"Why not?"

"Well, because you live in Sydney for a start. Your work is in Sydney and I have my degree to finish."

"You can transfer to Sydney," he countered, cool and logical. "I know people. I can pull some strings—"

"No." Both her hands came down on the table hard enough to rattle her plate. "You absolutely cannot pull strings. I got where I am on my own and I will continue to do so."

"Because you're too independent to accept help?"

"Because I value what comes from effort. Everything I have and everything I am comes from hard work."

His eyes narrowed slightly. "Unlike me?"

She met his eyes and knew, in her heart, she was doing him another injustice. But then she also recalled where this argument had started and how every argument ended with this kind of vehemence. "How can I marry you," she asked, "when every debate ends in this kind of frustration?"

"If we were married, perhaps we wouldn't be frustrated. At the cabin we got along just fine. Remember?"

"How can I forget?" she asked with a twisted smile. She remembered all the getting along just fine. "I also remember the first weekend at the cabin and our discussion about marrying for the right reason. Do you remember that?"

"I remember."

"Then you know that I don't believe two parents are necessarily better than one."

He stiffened so perceptively Zara swore she heard a snap. "Are you saying you want to raise this baby—*our baby*—alone?"

"I'd prefer if he or she—" she paused, overcome for an instant by the concept of this baby as a boy or a girl, as a real, living, breathing baby "—if our baby has two involved parents. But I don't believe they need to be married."

"You'd rather live together?"

"I'd rather we reach some agreement for shared custody—"

"No. That's not the best thing for a child, being tossed between two homes."

Zara lifted her hands, palms up, in a helpless gesture. "See? We can't agree on anything. I told you the last time we talked why I couldn't handle a relationship with you. None of that has changed just because I'm pregnant."

He looked away, and she could see the flick of a tensed muscle at the corner of his jaw for the second before he turned back. "Think about it, Zara. Think about how much easier it would be for everyone if we married. As my wife you won't have to worry about what the papers say about you. Have you thought about that? About what happens if they latch on to the fact that you're pregnant and I'm the father?"

No, she hadn't. Zara's stomach churned. How could she have not realized that?

"Marry me, Zara, and I'll protect you from all that. You'll have the best medical care and afterward we can hire a nanny. You can study, you can work, you can have whatever you want."

And that last phrase lodged in Zara's chest, thick and unshakable. Yes, he could give her opportunities and care and everything money could buy. Yes, his name and his position might protect her on some level, once the tabloids had their initial fun dragging her through the mire.

But sitting there at her little kitchen table listening to his deep voice and his fervent promises only made her realize the one thing he hadn't mentioned. The only thing that mattered and the only thing that could make a marriage work.

He hadn't mentioned love.

"I'm sorry, Alex, but I can't marry you," she said quietly. "I don't believe you can give me what I want."

Thirteen

Alex had thought he couldn't marry a woman who didn't want him. He recalled telling Zara those exact words the weekend he'd met her. Yet in the days after she turned him down—after she turned his world upside down—he discovered that he'd lied.

He wanted to marry Zara Lovett, despite her rejection. He wanted to marry her even after she'd looked him in the eye and coolly told him he couldn't give her what she wanted. He didn't have to ask her to elucidate.

He remembered her exact words when they'd first discussed marriage, that same night at the cabin. She'd told him she would only marry a man she wanted to share her whole life with. Someone she couldn't bear living without.

Obviously he wasn't that man and she was not prepared to take anything less.

And, dammit, he wasn't going to beg. Nor was he laying his pride out for her to stomp all over again.

But that didn't mean he was about to give up. He wanted her as his wife; he wanted his child's parents together, preferably married, before the birth. He just had to work out a plan to make it so.

For now he'd agreed to give her the time and space she'd requested to get through her end-of-year exams. After much pressing, she'd finally thrown her hands in the air and agreed to accept his financial help immediately, since she'd had to resign her job at Personal Best. But she refused his proposal to send his housekeeper/cook to look after her and his offer to buy her a car.

The second was nonnegotiable. He would buy her a car. She just didn't know it yet.

She had, however, relented on a couple of key issues.

At first she'd not wanted anyone else to know until she was further along in the pregnancy, since things could go wrong, but then she'd conceded that his mother and brothers should know because of the will.

Secondly, she'd agreed to him accompanying her on her first prenatal visit, after she'd finished her exams. That had surprised him. Perhaps she'd seen the obdurate set of his jaw or perhaps he'd swayed her with his reminder that this was *their* baby.

"I will let you know once I've made an appointment," she'd told him, and Alex had dipped his head in acknowledgment. "I appreciate that. Thank you, Zara."

He knew that was the only way to make any ground with her. With polite, controlled, nonconfrontational exchanges. He knew and yet he'd struggled—each time he'd called her since—to keep the heat of frustration from his voice.

He'd struggled, too, against the impulse to ask all kinds of incendiary questions. When he asked how she was feeling, he wanted to then ask if her body was changing. If she felt any different. Did she ever lie awake at night thinking that this was *his* baby inside her, a part of him that would forever bond them together, whether she wished it or not?

He wanted to remind her of the other nights they'd talked on the phone, when they'd laughed and shared details of their days, when she'd sighed and told him she missed him in her bed.

But these conversations were short and awkward, punctuated with fraught silences and always ending with her saying she needed to get back to work.

Tonight Alex had called with a purpose beyond asking after her health. He'd invited her to Kameruka Downs to meet his family the weekend after her exams finished and, dammit, he'd felt as tongue-tied as a teenager asking a girl out for the first time.

The silence after he finally got his tongue around the invitation felt damningly thick.

"I want you to meet Mau," he said stiffly. "My mother. And she will want to meet you."

"Have you told her yet?" she asked. "About the baby."

"This weekend, I'll tell her then."

"Will the rest of your family be there?"

"Yes. Tomas's wife is throwing a small party for Cat. Rate's wife. This will be her first visit, too. I thought that might help. You won't be the only new—" God, he almost said *wife* but stopped himself in time and pinched the bridge of his nose "—newcomer."

"I don't think so," she said after a brief pause. "This is your sister-in-law's party."

Alex gripped his phone tighter. For some reason, without even knowing it, he'd been banking on her accepting. Banking on getting her out into the country where they might recapture a glimpse of what they'd shared at the cabin. A place where she would be comfortable and relaxed, where he could show her how it could be between them. "It's not like that," he told her, pacing the room, trying to control his gathering frustration. "Angie throws a party at the drop of a hat. It's no big deal. Just an excuse to dress up and invite a few neighbors over."

"I thought those outback neighbors were hundreds of miles away."

"They fly in."

He heard a sound that could have been laughter, but it was too short and sharp to tell. "Alex, I appreciate the invitation. And I do want to meet your family one day. But by this weekend I'm going to be exhausted. I'll only want to sleep."

"We have beds at Kameruka Downs."

She sighed and he could actually picture her tired face, her worn-out eyes from that day in her kitchen, and he felt a pressure in his chest. A pain born of helplessness because he could do nothing for her. She wouldn't let him. "Look, I have to go. I have studying—"

"To do," he finished over the top of her. "I know, Zara. I've heard it before."

And this time he didn't even bother telling her not to work too hard, to look after herself, to get some sleep. He knew that was a waste of breath. And after they'd said their stilted goodbyes, after she'd reminded him of the time of her doctor's appointment next week, he allowed himself to consider if he was also wasting his time and his hopes.

She didn't love him. She wouldn't marry him. How the hell did he think he could change that?

Alex didn't tell anyone about the baby straight off. At the back of his mind he'd been wondering about his sisters-in-law. Waiting for some announcement, he supposed, but so far there'd been nothing. If either Angie or Cat was pregnant, they sure weren't showing the same signs as Zara.

He heard Angie's distinctive laughter and turned to see her, the life of the party, surrounded by a group of neighbors. Mostly male. He smiled, but as always lately, the gesture felt tight and the smile didn't stick. He did feel a degree of satisfaction, however, when he noticed that Tomas was one of the group. And that he—his formerly morose little brother—had a grin as wide as the north all over his face.

Angie was good for him. But she looked the same as the last time he'd seen her, strong and healthy and vibrant. If she was pregnant, she sure as hell wasn't suffering.

Turning a slow half circle, he scanned the small assembly in the central courtyard of the sprawling homestead that was now Tomas and Angie's home, until he located his other sister in-law. Catriona. He found her sitting in a quiet corner, head bent toward Mau, listening intently.

Rafe had told him how she'd resisted making this trip for the two months since they'd married, how shy she'd been of meeting all the Carlisles, but finally he'd talked her into this weekend. Alex had wondered if that was significant. But then he couldn't imagine Rafe keeping quiet about anything, let alone impending fatherhood.

Right on cue, he felt a familiar thump between the shoulder blades.

"That's my wife you're ogling," Rafe said. "Do I need to punch your lights out?"

Alex snorted. "You could try."

They both watched Rafe's wife a second longer.

"She seems to be getting along fine with Mau."

"Are you thinking Dad knew what he was doing?"

Alex swirled the contents of the glass he'd forgotten he was holding. Whiskey. The color of Zara's eyes. The knowledge tightened his chest as he considered Rafe's question. "We assumed he wanted to see Mau happy again." He dipped his glass in that direction. "She's smiling now."

"My wife has that effect."

The tightness in Alex's chest constricted further at those words. *My wife.* As he noted the proprietary look on Rafe's face.

"The deadline's past," he noted. The three months they'd been granted to conceive, according to Chas's will.

"Don't take it too hard." Rafe cut him a look. "Tomas and I both consider we've won even though we've missed out on the inheritance."

"Neither of you?"

"Nope."

"Are you sure?"

"Pretty much."

Alex considered the depths of his whiskey another second. Cleared his throat. "I have some news."

Alex felt his brother's gaze shift and fix on his face. "Jeez, Alex, don't tell us you've been jilted again."

As far as jabs went, that one was pretty effective. And Rafe didn't even have a clue. Alex huffed out a breath and then looked up to meet his brother's eyes. "It seems I've made the deadline."

Rafe stared. The realization came slowly, in degrees, sharpening his gaze and curving his lips into a smile. "You sly dog." He slapped Alex on the back and then turned and called out across the courtyard. "Hey, little bro. Get over here."

Everyone turned and looked. Rafe grinned and shook his head. "I did not see that one coming."

* * *

Alex ushered his brothers inside, before Rafe decided to yell the news to all and sundry. In the office where this had all started the afternoon they'd buried their father, he told them that Zara was pregnant and that for the moment that news stayed within these walls.

"She hasn't even seen a doctor yet."

"But she's sure she's pregnant?" Tomas asked. "Those home tests can be—"

"She's sure. She's studying medicine. She knows the symptoms."

Tomas whistled. "A doctor. Nice."

Rafe grinned. "Seems big brother's been checking out her bedside manner."

Alex ignored his brothers' ribbing. He knew he should feel some measure of satisfaction. He'd fulfilled the terms of the will. He'd carried out Chas's last wish.

But even when Tomas unearthed his father's aged Glenfiddich to toast Alex's success, he felt no joy. When Rafe made a second toast to the first Carlisle grandchild—"I'm going to be an uncle!"—Alex's smile was forced.

And when he turned and saw his mother in the doorway, when he felt the shrewd sharpness of her eyes on his face, he knew she hadn't missed a thing.

"Rafe. Tomas." Mau's gaze didn't veer. "I would like to speak with Alexander in private."

They left without demur. When their mother used a name in full, they knew she meant business.

"You have some news to tell me?"

Mau hadn't been privy to the added clause in her husband's will and when she'd found out she'd been ropable. She looked no happier now as Alex repeated what he'd told his brothers. A bare-bones version of how she was to become a grandmother.

"If everything goes well. Zara's only eight weeks along."

"Zara." She seemed to weigh the name on her tongue, even as she weighed the story he'd told. Perhaps what he hadn't. "How do you feel about this? You don't look very happy."

"I'm…" He huffed out a breath. Looked away as he battled a heart-ripping surge of emotion. And when he looked back up, he knew he couldn't even try to hide all he felt from his mother's keen eyes. "She won't marry me. She's independent and stubborn and she thinks she's better off on her own. I've offered her everything. I don't know what else I can do."

"Have you told her you love her?" Mau asked.

"Why do you assume I love her?"

"I pray that you do, seeing as you seem so set on marrying her."

"She's having my child. Of course I'm set on marrying her."

Mau shook her head sadly. "You should know better than that, Alexander. What do you think would have happened if I'd married your father? Or Rafe's? I was too young and lost to know what I wanted then, but at least I knew enough not to marry for the wrong reason."

He looked away again. Studied his untouched whiskey. Saw Zara's eyes and heard her voice telling him about the right reasons. About love. "And if I do love her?"

"I suggest you tell her so."

"What if she doesn't feel the same way?"

"Oh, Alex." She put her hand on his arm. Squeezed gently. "I know you guard your emotions tightly and I think I know why. But you're nothing like him, you know."

His biological father. Alex didn't have to ask.

"He was wild, he had a temper, and he never had the will to try and control it. You're strong, like your grandfather and like the man Charles raised you to be. Sometimes I think you're too strong-willed. Too set on keeping everything inside." She squeezed his arm again. "Don't let that make you unhappy. If you love her, Alex, you need to tell her."

"And if she doesn't want to hear it?"

"If she's the right woman, that's all she'll want to hear."

By Sunday afternoon, Zara had had enough of sleeping and recuperating from exam stress. Not that all that lounging about didn't have its advantages. For example, she hadn't thrown up since Friday morning. But on the other side of the coin, not thinking about cytology and urology and hematology meant she had too much thinking space for Alex.

Unable to sit around doing nothing, yet not sure she wanted to push herself too hard—she could get used to this not-throwing-up thing very easily—she searched for her knitting bag, last used in the winter when she'd knocked off a scarf for Tim and another for Mr. Krakowski next door. Luckily they both supported the same football team so she could use the same colors and pattern. Black and white stripes were not that complicated.

She rummaged through her bits and pieces but nothing inspired her. Then it struck her. The baby. She could make…she didn't know what. She didn't know what babies needed and that struck her as a huge hole in her education. Up until this weekend she'd been too busy and too sick, but suddenly she wanted to know. Suddenly she had time to go to town to look through the shops. To educate herself.

Three hours later, she didn't feel educated so much as overwhelmed. Wandering back from her tram stop, she was a little excited, a little fearful, and incredibly thankful that she'd not been too proud to accept Alex's financial help. Raising a baby, she had learned today, was a very expensive exercise.

Turning the corner into her street, she started searching for her keys. She'd almost reached her house before she found them and when she straightened she saw him. Alex. Standing by her gate as if he'd been watching her approach.

Her heart thudded painfully hard as she came to a dead stop. Dimly she felt the key chain slipping through her fingers and when she heard the metallic jangle of keys hitting concrete, she tightened her grip on her tote bag. It felt like that might be the only thing she had a grip on.

"Hello, Zara." His voice sounded different. Thick. But perhaps that was her hearing. He took a step closer and she thought, for one breathless second, that he was going to kiss her. But then he ducked down and picked up her keys. "You dropped these."

Disappointment flooded her veins. "What are you doing here?"

"Waiting for you."

She was pretty sure they'd had this conversation before. It felt eerily familiar. Zara frowned. "Weren't you going to Kameruka Downs this weekend?"

"I've been. This morning I decided to fly down here instead of back to Sydney."

"The doctor's appointment isn't until Tuesday."

"I know."

"Oh." And she stood there in the quiet Sunday afternoon sunshine just looking at him. Her heart still beat too hard to be healthy. All she could think was *How could I miss him this much?*

His thick dark hair was slightly ruffled, as if he'd been raking his fingers through it. His blue-gray eyes swirled with some emotion she couldn't pin down. The grooves in his cheeks looked deeper but she didn't think it was from too much smiling. She wanted to reach up and trace them.

Wanted to touch him so badly she started to shake.

"Here. Let me take your shopping," he said, perhaps afraid she'd keel over.

There was that danger. Then he reached for her bag and their hands tangled and brushed and oh, the heat. The charge. The catch in her chest that had to be her heart standing still.

"I'll get the door for you," he said, and she followed him through her tiny gate and up the two steps to her door. He leaned down and picked up something from the stoop, and looked back over his shoulder at her. "When you didn't answer the door, I was going to leave this."

This, she realized was a pot of flowers. She didn't know what kind, only that they were bright and beautiful and shaking very badly when he put them into her hands. "Thank you," she managed to say even though her throat was thick with emotion. "They're gorgeous."

Then they were back to staring at each other again, except this time he smiled and touched her cheek with the back of his hand. "You're looking good, Zara. Rested."

"Not like hell?"

"The opposite, actually." His smile faded. "Please. Can I come in? There's something I have to say to you."

He looked so grave, so serious that Zara felt a belated jolt of apprehension. "Is something wrong? Is someone—"

His touch stilled her, silenced her. A hand on her shoulder. The stroke of his thumb against her collarbone. "No. It's nothing like that. I just…" He sucked in a breath and she realized that he also looked nervous. "Can we go inside?"

"Yes. Yes, of course." She nodded toward the keys in his hand. "It's the second key. The gold one."

Inside, she ushered him to the sitting room where he'd waited for her the last time. The day he'd got it all wrong. He put down her bag on the red sofa and when she fussed about making tea, he stopped her with a hand on her shoulder. This time he didn't let go. This time he turned her toward him and looked into her face.

"Unless you need that cup of tea desperately, I'd like you to stay. To listen." If he didn't say this now, they'd end up sidetracked and arguing. "I've been thinking about us. And about the last time I saw you. What I said and what I didn't say. I got it all wrong, Zara."

She moistened her lips. Said nothing. In her throat he could see the beat of her pulse and touched it with his thumb.

"What I should have said…what I wanted to say…what I think you needed me to say…"

"Yes?" she prompted.

And there was something hopeful in her tone. Something in the depths of those beautiful eyes that steadied the wild jangle of his nerves and gave him the words he needed. Gave him the confidence to do this right. His hand slid down her arm until he held her hand in his. Then he went down on one knee.

"Zara Lovett, I want you to be my wife. Not because you're going to be the mother of my baby. Not because I have this primal need to take care of you and it makes me crazy thinking that you're sick and I'm not here to help. Not because I want you in my bed every night or because you still have to teach me that smooth fishing cast."

His thumb stroked over her knuckles and he tightened his grip.

"I want you for my wife because I love you and want to spend the rest of my life with you. Will you marry me, Zara?"

For a long second she said nothing. She moistened her lips. She drew a breath that snagged in her throat, possibly because it felt like her heart was there. Crazy-dancing high in her chest.

Could she believe him? Oh, but she wanted to, so badly. He sounded sincere, but was this only to get his own way? Had he gone away and remembered what she'd told him about marriage? Is that why he'd gotten it so right—because she had supplied the lines?

"I'm on my knees here. Please, say yes."

He tugged on her hand, until she gave in and came down to his level. "How can this work, Alex? I don't know—"

"We can make it work," he said fiercely. "If we want it badly enough."

"There are things you don't know about me."

"You snore? Sweetheart, I know that. I've slept with you already."

She punched his shoulder lightly and he grabbed her fisted hand and kissed the knuckles, one by one. If she weren't already on her knees, that would have done the trick.

"Is this secret about Susannah?" he asked. "And your father?"

She sucked in a breath, her eyes wide. "You knew? How?"

"I didn't know for sure, until now."

"You guessed?" Her voice rose a semitone. "How?"

"An educated guess. I told you I'd like your sister." He smiled. "And I do. She introduced us, in a roundabout way."

Zara just stared, completely undone.

"And, please, don't say anything else about your mother

or your father or the scandal that might cause. If you marry me, you will be my wife. They can say what they like, it won't change the fact that I love you."

"I still want to finish my degree," she said.

"Of course you do. I can live wherever I like. Wherever *you* like."

"You would move?" she asked in hushed wonder. "To Melbourne?"

"If that's what you want."

Slowly she shook her head. "Why would you do that?"

"Because I love you. To be together."

She blinked rapidly, to ward off the emotion brimming in her eyes. And then she couldn't help herself. She had to put her hands on him, cupping his face. "You really do."

He smiled, and she leaned in and kissed him on that smile, drinking its happiness into her body. Feeling it wash through her in a wave of bliss. "I love you, too, Alex. I had no idea how much until right now."

His eyes closed for a second, and when they opened they were full of everything she was feeling. She touched her thumb to his mouth, traced the bow of his top lip. Kissed him again.

"Is that a yes?" he asked.

"Yes. That is definitely a yes."

Zara let that sink in a moment. The fact that she had just agreed to marry him. The fact that despite her happiness, the concept of marriage still scared her some. Then he smiled at her and that shadow of fear faded to black.

"I did you another disservice," she said.

"Oh?" His hands slid up her arms, then over her shoulders and down her back. As though he were learning her shape all over again.

"I thought I couldn't love you because you weren't a man I could have taken home to meet my mother."

He stopped with his hands on her waist, his expression slightly affronted. "I would have loved to meet your mother. And she would have loved me."

Zara raised her brows. "How do you figure that?"

"Because I'm going to love her daughter so well." His hands slid lower until they cupped her hips. "And spoil her rotten by giving her whatever she wants." He tugged her forward until their bodies touched. "And make her so damn satisfied she won't ever stop smiling."

She was smiling when he started to kiss her, and smiling even broader when he finished a long time later. Slowly her eyes drifted open and she snuggled against him, loving the feel of his body against hers. "Tell me about your house."

"What do you want to know?"

"Just…what it's like."

"It's like a house." Alex shrugged. "Walls, roof. Lots of rooms inside."

She laughed, amused and delighted by that answer. "Does it have a pool?"

"Two."

"Are you joshing me?"

"One outdoor, one indoor." Then perhaps misinterpreting why she'd gone still, he said, "We can fill one in if you think that's excessive."

"Does it have a gym?" she asked after another moment.

"It has a first-rate gym," he answered solemnly, and his hands slid under her shirt and peeled it from her body. "Now, is there anything else you want to know about my house? Because in about sixty seconds—" he unhooked her bra "—I'm not going to be able to talk."

"Oh, why's that?"

He pulled her bra off and tossed it. "My mouth is going to be otherwise occupied."

"So," she said some time later, when she'd regained her breath. They were in her bed, naked, sated. Happy. "How far is this house from Sydney University?"

Alex opened one eye. "Does this mean we're going to live in Sydney?"

"Possibly. Although I want you to know that this isn't to set a precedent. You will not always get your own way."

Alex just smiled and hugged her body close against his and started planning when he would next have his way with her.

Epilogue

Zara did move into Alex's Sydney home and she decided they would keep both pools. The gym was, indeed, first rate and Alex had his way with her several memorable times within its mirrored, equipment-packed walls.

He did not get his way over a quick wedding, however.

Zara refused to rush into marriage and insisted on a six-month cooling-down period. Things did not cool down and they were married in the courtyard of Kameruka Downs under the broad blue northern sky.

Rafe was Alex's best man, which gave him license to drop all kinds of lines about being the best man. Susannah returned from America in time to act as maid of honor, and although she remained quietly mysterious about her man she completed Zara's happiness by letting everyone know she was the bride's sister.

Angie, of course, organized the reception party for family and a small group of friends. Catriona was supposed to help her with the food except her delicate early-pregnancy stomach objected to the first whiff of seafood. Angie smiled and patted her mini-bulge and thanked whatever fates had made her so hale and hearty.

Maura Keane Carlisle sat in the front row for the ceremony, holding Tomas's hand tightly and smiling broadly despite the stream of tears coursing down her face.

And from up above "King" Carlisle looked down on them all and smiled. His beloved wife and his three boys, all happy, all smiling. His mission was accomplished.

* * * * *

If you enjoyed what you just read,
then we've got an offer you can't resist!

Take 2 bestselling
love stories FREE!

Plus get a FREE surprise gift!

Clip this page and mail it to Silhouette Reader Service™

IN U.S.A.	**IN CANADA**
3010 Walden Ave.	P.O. Box 609
P.O. Box 1867	Fort Erie, Ontario
Buffalo, N.Y. 14240-1867	L2A 5X3

YES! Please send me 2 free Silhouette Desire® novels and my free surprise gift. After receiving them, if I don't wish to receive anymore, I can return the shipping statement marked cancel. If I don't cancel, I will receive 6 brand-new novels every month, before they're available in stores! In the U.S.A., bill me at the bargain price of $3.80 plus 25¢ shipping and handling per book and applicable sales tax, if any*. In Canada, bill me at the bargain price of $4.47 plus 25¢ shipping and handling per book and applicable taxes**. That's the complete price and a savings of at least 10% off the cover prices—what a great deal! I understand that accepting the 2 free books and gift places me under no obligation ever to buy any books. I can always return a shipment and cancel at any time. Even if I never buy another book from Silhouette, the 2 free books and gift are mine to keep forever.

225 SDN DZ9F
326 SDN DZ9G

Name	(PLEASE PRINT)	
Address	Apt.#	
City	State/Prov.	Zip/Postal Code

Not valid to current Silhouette Desire® subscribers.

Want to try two free books from another series?
Call 1-800-873-8635 or visit www.morefreebooks.com.

 * Terms and prices subject to change without notice. Sales tax applicable in N.Y.
** Canadian residents will be charged applicable provincial taxes and GST.
   All orders subject to approval. Offer limited to one per household.
   ® are registered trademarks owned and used by the trademark owner or its licensee.

DES04R   ©2004 Harlequin Enterprises Limited

eHARLEQUIN.com

The Ultimate Destination for Women's Fiction

Calling all aspiring writers!
Learn to craft the perfect romance novel
with our useful tips and tools:

- Take advantage of our **Romance Novel Critique Service** for detailed advice from romance professionals.

- Use our **message boards** to connect with writers, published authors and editors.

- Enter our **Writing Round Robin**— you could be published online!

- Learn many tools of the writer's trade from editors and authors in our **On Writing** section!

- **Writing guidelines** for Harlequin or Silhouette novels—what our editors *really* look for.

Learn more about romance writing from the experts—
visit www.eHarlequin.com today!

The colder the winter, the sweeter the blackberries will be once spring arrives.

**Will the Kimball women discover
the promise of a beautiful spring?**

Blackberry
WINTER
Cheryl REAVIS

HARLEQUIN®

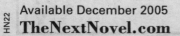

Silhouette® Desire

COMING NEXT MONTH

#1693 NAME YOUR PRICE—Barbara McCauley
Dynasties: The Ashtons
His family's money and power tore them apart, but will time be able to heal the wounds of this priceless love?

#1694 TRUST ME—Caroline Cross
Men of Steele
An ex-navy SEAL is in over his head when he has to rescue the woman who broke his heart years ago.

#1695 A MOST SHOCKING REVELATION—Kristi Gold
Texas Cattleman's Club: The Secret Diary
A sexy sheriff is torn between his duty and his desire for a woman looking for her own brand of justice.

#1696 A BRIDE BY CHRISTMAS—Joan Elliott Pickart
Is this wedding planner really cursed never to find true love—or has Mr. Right just not appeared…until now?

#1697 TYCOON TAKES REVENGE—Anna DePalo
An infamous playboy gives a gossip columnist a taste of her own medicine, but finds that love is far sweeter than revenge.

#1698 TROPHY WIVES—Jan Colley
What will this wounded millionaire find beneath this rich girl's carefree facade?